I'M WITH THE BEARS

I'M WITH THE BEARS

MARGARET ATWOOD

PAOLO BACIGALUPI

T. C. BOYLE

TOBY LITT

LYDIA MILLET

DAVID MITCHELL

NATHANIEL RICH

KIM STANLEY ROBINSON

HELEN SIMPSON

WU MING 1

Introduced by Bill McKibben

Edited by Mark Martin

VERSO

London • New York

Verso
UK: 6 Meard Street, London W1F 0EG
US: 20 Jay Street, Suite 1010, Brooklyn, NY 11201
www.versobooks.com

Verso is the imprint of New Left Books

ISBN-13: 978-1-84467-744-3

British Library Cataloguing in Publication Data
A catalogue record for this book is available from the British Library

Library of Congress Cataloging-in-Publication Data
A catalog record for this book is available from the Library of Congress

Typeset in Electra by Hewer UK Ltd, Edinburgh

Printed in the US by Maple Vail

John Muir said that if it ever came to a war between the races, he would side with the bears. That day has arrived.

—Dave Foreman,
"Strategic Monkeywrenching"

CONTENTS

CONTENTS

INTRODUCTION

by Bill McKibben

The problem with writing about global warming may be that the truth is larger than usually makes for good fiction. It's pure pulp. Consider the recent past—consider a single year, 2010. It's the warmest year on record (though not, of course, for long). Nineteen nations set new all-time temperature records—in Pakistan, in June, the all-time mark for the entire continent of Asia fell, when the mercury hit 128 degrees.

And heat like that has Technicolor effects. In the Arctic, ice melt galloped along—both the northwest and northeast passages were open for the first time in history, and there was an impromptu yacht race through terrain where even a decade before no one had ever imagined humans being able to travel. In Russia, the heat rose like some inverse of Dr. Zhivago; instead of the Ice Palace, huge walls of flame as the peat bogs around Moscow burned without cease. The temperature had

1

never hit a hundred degrees in the capital but it topped that mark eight times in August; the drought was so deep that the Kremlin stopped all grain exports to the rest of the world, pushing the price of wheat through the roof (and contributing at least a portion to the unrest that gripped countries like Tunisia and Egypt).

And in Pakistan? Oh good God. Here's how it works: warm air holds more water vapor than cold, so the atmosphere is about four percent moister than it was forty years ago. This loads the dice for deluge and downpour, and in late July of 2010 Pakistan threw snake eyes: in the mountains, which in a normal year average three feet of rain, twelve feet fell *in a week*. The Indus swelled till it covered a quarter of the nation, an area the size of Britain. It was the first of at least six megafloods that stretched into the early months of 2011, and some were even more dramatic—in Queensland, Australia a landscape larger than France and Germany was inundated. But Pakistan—oh good God. Six months later four million people were still homeless. And of course they were people who had done literally nothing to cause this cataclysm—they hadn't been pouring carbon into the atmosphere.

That's our job—that's what we do in the West. And it's why a book like this is of such potential importance. Somehow we have to summon up the courage to act. Because here's the math: everything that I described above, all the carnage of 2010, comes with one degree of global warming. It's a taste of the early stages of global warming—but only the early stages. Scientists tell us with robust consensus that unless we act very soon (much sooner than is economically or politically conven-ient) that one degree will be four or five degrees before the century is out. If one degree melts the Arctic, put your poetic license to work. Your imagination is the limit; as one NASA research team put it in 2008, unless we reduce the amount of carbon in the atmosphere quickly, we can't have a planet "compatible with the one on which civilization developed and to which life on earth is adapted."

So far our efforts to do anything substantial about that truth have been thwarted, completely. The fossil fuel indus-try has won every single battle, usually with some version of this argument: doing anything about climate change will cause short-term economic pain. And since we can under-stand and imagine the anguish of short-term economic pain (think of the ink spilled, and with good reason, over the reces-sion of the last few years) we make it a priority. Since global warming seems, almost by definition, hard to imagine (after all, it's never happened before) it gets short shrift. Until that changes, we'll take none of the actions that might ameliorate our plight.

And here science can take us only so far. The scientists have done their job—they've issued every possible warning, flashed every red light. Now it's time for the rest of us—for the economists, the psychologists, the theologians. And the artists, whose role is to help us understand what things *feel* like. These stories are an impressive start in that direction, and one shouldn't forget for a moment that they represent a real departure from most literary work. Instead of being consumed with the relationships between people, they increasingly take on the relationship between people and everything else. On a stable planet, nature provided a background against which the human drama took place; on the unstable planet we're creating, *the background becomes the highest drama.* So many of these pieces conjure up that world, and a tough world it is, not the familiar one we've loved without even thinking of it. Those are jolts we dearly need; this is serious business we're involved in.

But to shift, of course, the human heart requires not just fear but hope. And so one task, perhaps, of our letters in this emergency is to help provide that sense of what life might be like in the world past fossil fuel. Not just a bleak sense, but a bright one; a glimpse of what a future might look like where community begins to replace consumption. It's not impossibly farfetched—even in the desperate last decade, the number of farms in the U.S. rose for the first time in a century and a half, as people discovered the farmer's market, and as a new generation started to learn the particular pleasures and responsibilities that most of mankind once knew on a daily basis; in that sense, we've had writers like Wendell Berry who have been working this ground for a long time.

Of course, in the end, the job of writers is not to push us in some particular direction; it's to illuminate. To bear witness. With climate change we face the biggest single thing human beings have ever done, so big as to be almost invisible. By pointing it out, the world's writers help pose the question for the final exam humanity now faces: was the big brain adaptive, or not? Clearly it can get us into considerable hot water. In the next few years we'll find out whether that big brain, hopefully attached to a big heart, can get us out.

2011

THE SISKIYOU, JULY 1989

by T. C. Boyle

This is the way it begins, on a summer night so crammed with stars the Milky Way looks like a white plastic sack strung out across the roof of the sky. No moon, though—that wouldn't do at all. And no sound, but for the discontinuous trickle of water, the muted patter of cheap tennis sneakers on the ghostly surface of the road and the sustained applause of the crickets. It's a dirt road, a logging road, in fact, but Tyrone Tierwater wouldn't want to call it a road. He'd call it a scar, a gash, an open wound in the body corporal of the forest. But for the sake of convenience, let's identify it as a road. In daylight, trucks pound over it, big D7 Cats, loaders, wood-chippers. It's a road. And he's on it.

He's moving along purposively, all but invisible in the abyss of shadow beneath the big Douglas firs. If your eyes were adjusted to the dark and you looked closely enough, you might detect his three companions, the night disarranging itself ever so casually as they pass: now you see them, now you don't. All four are dressed identically, in cheap tennis sneakers blackened with shoe polish, two pairs of socks, black tees and sweatshirts, and, of course, the black watchcaps. Where would they be without them?

Tierwater had wanted to go further, the whole nine yards, stripes of greasepaint down the bridge of the nose, slick rays of it fanning out across their cheekbones—or better yet, blackface—but Andrea talked him out of it. She can talk him out of anything, because she's more rational than he, more aggressive, because she has a better command of the language and eyes that bark after weakness like hounds—but then she doesn't have half his capacity for paranoia, neurotic display, pessimism or despair. Things can go wrong. They do. They will. He tried to tell her that, but she wouldn't listen.

They were back in the motel room at the time, on the unfledged strip of the comatose town of Grants Pass, Oregon, where they were registered under the name of Mr. and Mrs. James Watt. He was nervous—butterflies in the stomach, termites in the head—nervous and angry. Angry at the loggers, Oregon, the motel room, her. Outside, three steps from the door, Teo's Chevy Caprice (anonymous gray, with the artfully smudged plates) sat listing in its appointed slot. He came out of the bathroom with a crayon in one hand, a glittering, shrink-wrapped package of Halloween face paint in the other. There were doughnuts on the bed in a staved-in carton, paper coffee cups subsiding into the low fiberboard table. "Forget it, Ty," she said. "I keep telling you, this is nothing, the first jab in a whole long bout. You think I'd take Sierra along if I wasn't a hundred percent sure it was safe? It's going to be a stroll in the park, it is."

A moment evaporated. He looked at his daughter, but she had nothing to say, her head cocked in a way that indicated she was listening, but only reflexively. The TV said, "—and these magnificent creatures, their range shrinking, can no longer find the mast to sustain them, let alone the carrion." He tried to smile, but the appropriate muscles didn't seem to be working. He had misgivings about the whole business, especially when it came to Sierra—but as he stood there listening to the insects sizzle against the bug zapper outside the window, he understood that "misgivings" wasn't exactly the word he wanted. Misgivings? How about crashing fears, terrors, night-sweats? The inability to swallow? A heart ground up like glass?

There were people out there who weren't going to like what the four of them were planning to do to that road he didn't want to call a road. Bosses, under-bosses, heavy machine operators, CEOs, power-lunchers, police, accountants. Not to mention all those good, decent, hard-working and terminally misguided timber families, the men in baseball caps and red suspenders, the women like tented houses, people who spent their spare time affixing loops of yellow ribbon to every shrub, tree, doorknob, mailbox and car antenna in every town up and down the coast. They had mortgages, trailers, bass boats, plans for the future, and the dirt-blasted bumpers of their pickups sported stickers that read *Save a Skunk, Roadkill an Activist* and *Do You Work for a Living or Are You an Environmentalist?*

They were angry—born angry—and they didn't much care about physical restraint, one way or the other. Talk about misgivings—his daughter is only thirteen years old, for all her Gothic drag and nose ring and the cape of hair that drapes her shoulders like an advertisement, and she's never participated in an act of civil disobedience in her life, not even a daylit rally with minicams whirring and a supporting cast of thousands. "Come on," he pleaded, "just under the eyes, then. To mask the glow."

Andrea just shook her head. She looked good in black, he had to admit it, and the watchcap, riding low over her eyebrows, was a very sexy thing. They'd been married three months now, and everything about her was a novelty and a revelation, right down to the way she stepped into her jeans in the morning or pouted over a saucepan of ratatouille, a thin strip of green pepper disappearing between her lips while the steam rose witchily in her hair. "What if the police pull us over?" she said. "Ever think of that? What're you going to say— 'The game really ran late tonight, officer'? Or 'Gee, it was a great old-timey minstrel show—you should have been there.' " She was the one with the experience here—she was the organizer, the protestor, the activist—and she wasn't giving an inch. "The trouble with you," she said, running a finger under the lip of her cap, "is you've been watching too many movies."

Maybe so. But you couldn't really call the proposition relevant, not now, not here. This is the wilderness, or what's left of it. The night is deep, the road intangible, the stars the feeblest mementos of the birth of the universe. There are nine galaxies out there for each person alive today, and each of those galaxies features 100 billion suns, give or take the odd billion, and yet he can barely see where he's going, groping like a sleepwalker, one foot stabbing after the other. This is crazy, he's thinking, this is trouble, like stumbling around in a cave waiting for the bottom to fall out. He's wondering if the others are having as hard a time as he is, thinking vaguely about beta carotene supplements and night-vision goggles, when an owl chimes in somewhere ahead of them, a single wavering cry that says it has something strangled in its claws.

His daughter, detectable only through the rhythmic snap of her gum, asks in a theatrical whisper if that could be a spotted owl, "I mean hopefully, by any chance?"

He can't see her face, the night a loose-fitting jacket, his mind ten miles up the road, and he answers before he can think: "Don't I wish."

Right beside him, from the void on his left, another voice weighs in, the voice of Andrea, his second wife, the wife who is not Sierra's biological mother and so free to take on the role of her advocate in all disputes, tiffs, misunderstandings, misrepresentations and adventures gone wrong: "Give the kid a break, Ty." And then, in a whisper so soft it's like a feather floating down out of the night, "Sure it is, honey, that's a spotted owl if ever I heard one."

Tierwater keeps walking, the damp working odor of the nighttime woods in his nostrils, the taste of it on his tongue—mold transposed to another element, mold ascendant—but he's furious suddenly. He doesn't like this. He doesn't like it at

11

all. He knows it's necessary, knows the woods are being raped and the world stripped right on down to the last twig and that somebody's got to save it, but still he doesn't like it. His voice, cracking with the strain, leaps out ahead of him: "Keep it down, will you? We're supposed to be stealthy here—this is illegal, what we're doing, remember? Christ, you'd think we were on a nature walk or something, *And here's where the woodpecker lives, and here the giant forest fern.*"

A chastened silence, into which the crickets pour all their Orthopteran angst, but it can't hold. One more voice enters the mix, an itch of the larynx emanating from the vacancy to his right. This is Teo, Teo Van Sparks, a.k.a. Liverhead. Eight years ago he was standing out on Rodeo Drive, in front of Sterling's Fur Emporium, with a slab of calf's liver sutured to his shaved head. He'd let the liver get ripe—three or four days or so, flies like a crown of thorns, maggots beginning to trail down his nose—and then he'd tear it off his head and lay it at the feet of a silvery old crone in chinchilla or a starlet parading through the door in white fox. Next day he'd be back again, with a fresh slab of meat. Now he's a voice on the EF! circuit (*Eco-Agitator*, that's what his card says), thirty-one years old, a weightlifter with the biceps, triceps, lats and abs to prove it, and there isn't anything about the natural world he doesn't know. At least not that he'll admit. "Sorry, kids," he says, "but by most estimates they're down to less than five hundred breeding pairs in the whole range, from BC down to the Southern Sierra, so I doubt—"

"Fewer," Andrea corrects, in her pedantic mode. She's in charge here tonight, and she's going to rein them all in, right on down to the finer points of English grammar and usage. If it was just a question of giving out instructions in a methodical, dispassionate voice, that would be one thing—but she's so supercilious, so self-satisfied, cocky, bossy. He's not sure he can take it. Not tonight.

"Fewer, right. So what I'm saying is, more likely it's your screech or flammulated or even your great gray. Of course, we'd have to hear its call to be sure. The spotted's a high-pitched hoot, usually in groups of fours or threes, very fast, crescendoing."

"Call, why don't you," Sierra whispers, and the silence of the night is no silence at all but the screaming backdrop to some imminent and catastrophic surprise. "So you can make it call back. Then we'll know, right?"

Is it his imagination, or can he feel the earth slipping out from under him? He's blind, totally blind, his shoulders hunched in anticipation of the first furtive blow, his breath coming hard, his heart hammering at the walls of its cage. And the others? They're moving down the road in a horizontal line like tourists on a pier, noisy and ambling, heedless. "And while we're at it," he says, and he's surprised by his own voice, the vehemence of it, "I just want to know one thing from you, Andrea—did you remember the diapers? Or is this going to be another in a long line of, of—"

"At what?"

"It. The subject of stealth and preparedness."

He's talking to nothing, to the void in front of him, moving down the invisible road and releasing strings of words like a street-gibberer. The owl sounds off again, and then something else, a rattling harsh buzz in the night.

"Of course I remembered the diapers." The reassuring thump of his wife's big mannish hand patting the cross-stitched nylon of her daypack. "And the sandwiches and granola bars and sunblock too. You think I don't know what I'm doing here? Is that what you're implying?"

He's implying nothing, but he's half a beat from getting excruciatingly specific. The honeymoon is over. He's out here risking arrest, humiliation, physical abuse and worse—and for her, all for her, or because of her, anyway—and her tone irritates him. He wants to come back at her, draw some blood, get a good old-fashioned domestic dispute going, but instead he lets the silence speak for him.

"What kind of sandwiches?" Sierra wants to know, a hushed and tremulous little missive inserted in the envelope of her parents' bickering. He can just make out the moving shape of her, black against black, the sloped shoulders, the too-big feet, the burgeoning miracle of tofu-fed flesh, and this is where the panic closes in on him again. What if things turn nasty? What then?

"Something special for you, honey. A surprise, okay?"

"Tomato, avocado and sprouts on honey wheat-berry, don't spare the mayo?"

A low whistle from Andrea. "I'm not saying."

"Hummus—hummus and tabouleh on pita. Whole wheat pita."

"Not saying."

"Peanut butter-marshmallow? Nusspli?"

A stroll in the park, isn't that what she said? Sure, sure it is. And we're making so much racket we might as well be shooting off fireworks and beating a big bass drum into the bargain. What fun, huh? The family that monkeywrenches together stays together? But what if they are *listening? What if they got word ahead of time, somebody finked, ratted, spilled the beans, crapped us out?* "Look, really," he hears himself saying, trying to sound casual, but getting nowhere with that, "you've got to be quiet. I'm begging you—Andrea, come on. Sierra. Teo. Just for my peace of mind, if nothing else—"

Andrea's response is clear and resonant, a definitive non-whisper. "They don't have a watchman, I keep telling you that—so get a grip, Ty." A caesura. The crickets, the muffled tramp of sneakered feet, the faintest soughing of a night breeze in the doomed expanse of branch and bough. "Tomorrow night they will, though—you can bet on it."

It's ten miles in, and they've given themselves three and a half hours at a good brisk clip, no stops for rest or scholarly dissertations on dendrology or Strigidae calls, their caps pulled down tight, individual water rations riding their backs in bota bags as fat and supple as overfed babies. They're carrying plastic buckets, one apiece, the indestructible kind that come with five gallons of paint at Dunn & Edwards or Colortone. The buckets are empty, light as nothing, but tedious all the same, rubbing against their shins and slapping at the outside of his bad knee just over the indentation where the arthroscope went in, scuffing and squeaking in a fabricated, not-made-for-this-earth kind of way. But there's no talking, not any more, not once they reach the eight-mile mark, conveniently indicated by a tiny day-glo EF! sticker affixed to the black wall of a doomed Douglas fir—a tree that took root here five hundred years before Columbus brought the technological monster to a sunny little island in the Caribbean.

But Tierwater wouldn't want to preach. He'd just want to explain what happened that night, how it stuck in him like a barbed hook, like a bullet lodged too close to the bone to remove, and how it was the beginning, the real beginning, of everything to come.

All right.

It's still dark when they arrive, four-fifteen by his watch, and the concrete—all thirty bags of it—is there waiting for them, not ten feet off the road. Andrea is the one who locates it, with the aid of the softly glowing red cap of her flashlight—watchman or no, it would be crazy to go shining lights out here—and the red, she explains, doesn't kill your night vision like the full glare of the white. Silently, they haul the concrete up the road—all of them, even Sierra, though sixty pounds of dead weight is a real load for her. "Don't be ridiculous, Dad," she says when he asks if she's okay—or whispers, actually, whispers didactically—"because if Burmese peasants or coolies or whatever that hardly weigh more than I do can carry hundred and twenty pound sacks of rice from dawn to dusk for something like thirty-two cents a day, then I can lift this."

He wants to say something to relieve the tension no one but him seems to be feeling, something about the Burmese, but they're as alien to him as the headhunters of the Rajang Valley—don't some of them make thirty-six cents a day, the lucky ones?—and the best he can do is mutter "Be my guest" into the sleeve of his black sweatshirt. Then he's bending for the next bag, snatching it to his chest and rising out of his crouch like a weightlifter. The odd grunt comes to him out of the dark, and the thin whine of the first appreciative mosquitoes.

In addition to the concrete, there are two shovels and a pick-axe secreted in the bushes. Without a word, he takes up the pick, and once he gets his hands wrapped round that length of tempered oak, once he begins raising it above his head and slamming it down into the yielding flesh of the road, he feels better. The fact that the concrete and the tools were here in the first place is something to cheer about—they have allies in this, confederates, grunts and foot soldiers—and he lets the knowledge of that soothe him, his shoulders working, breath coming in ragged gasps. The night compresses. The pick lifts and drops. He could be anywhere, digging a petunia bed, a root cellar, a grave, and he's beginning to think he's having an out-of-body experience when Andrea takes hold of his rising arm. "That's enough, Ty," she whispers.

Then it's the shovels. He and Teo take turns clearing the loose dirt from the trench and heaving it into the bushes, and before long they have an excavation eighteen inches deep, two feet wide and twelve feet across, a neat black line spanning the narrowest stretch of the road in the roseate glow of Andrea's flashlight. It may not be much of a road by most standards, but still it's been surveyed, dozed, cleared and tamped flat, and it brings the machines to the trees. There's no question about it—the trucks have to be stopped, the line has to be drawn. Here. Right here. *Our local friends have chosen well,* he thinks, leaning on the shovel and gazing up into the night where two dark fortresses of rock, discernible now only as the absence of stars, crowd in over the road: block it here and there's no way around.

They're tired, all of them. Beat, exhausted, zombified. Though they dozed away the afternoon at the Rest Ye May Motel and fueled themselves with sugar-dipped doughnuts and reheated diner coffee, the hike, the unaccustomed labor and the lateness of the hour are beginning to take their toll. Andrea and Teo are off in the bushes, bickering over something in short, sharp explosions of breath that hit the air like body blows. Sierra, who has an opinion on everything, is uncharacteristically silent, a shadow perched on a rock at the side of the road—she may want to save the world, but not at this hour. He can hardly blame her. He's sapped too, feeling it in his hamstrings, his shoulders, his tender knee, and when he tries to focus on anything other than the stars, random spots and blotches float across his field of vision like paramecia frolicking under the lens of a microscope. But they're not done yet. Now it's the water. And again, their comrades-in-arms have chosen well: shut your eyes and listen. That's right. That sound he's been hearing isn't the white noise of traffic on a freeway or the hiss of a stylus clogged with lint—it's water, the muted gargle of a stream passing into a conduit not fifty feet up the road. This is what the buckets are for—to carry the water to the trench and moisten the concrete. They're almost home.

But not quite. There seems to be some confusion about the concrete, the proportion of water to mix in, and have any of them—even he, son of a builder and thirty-nine years on this earth—ever actually worked with concrete? Have any of them built a wall, smoothed out a walk, set bricks? Teo once watched a pair of Mexican laborers construct a deck round the family pool, but he was a kid then and it was a long time ago. He thinks they just dumped the bags into a hand-cranked mixer and added water from the hose. Did they need a mixer, was that the problem? Andrea thinks she can recall setting fence-posts with her father on their ranch in Montana, and Tierwater has a vague recollection of watching his own father set charges of dynamite on one of his jobsites, stones flung up in the air and bang and bang again, but as far as concrete is concerned, he's drawing a blank. "I think we just dump the bags in the trench, level it out and add water to the desired consistency," he concludes with all the authority of a man who flunked chemistry twice.

Andrea is dubious. "Sounds like a recipe for cake batter."

Teo: "What consistency, though? This is quick-set stuff, sure, but if we get it too runny it's never going to set up in two hours, and that's all we've got."

A sigh of exasperation from Sierra. "I can't believe you guys—I mean three adults, and we come all the way out here, with all this planning and all, and nobody knows what they're doing? No wonder my generation is going to wind up inheriting a desert." He can hear the plaintive, plangent sound of her bony hands executing mosquitoes. "Plus, I'm tired. Really like monster-tired. I want to go home to bed."

He's giving it some thought. How hard could it be? The people who do this for a living—laying concrete, that is—could hardly be confused with geniuses. "What does it say on the package? Are there any directions?"

"Close one eye," Andrea warns, "because that way you don't lose all your night vision, just in case, I mean, if anybody—" and then she flicks on the flashlight. The world suddenly explodes in light, and it's a new world, dun-colored and circumscribed, sacks of concrete like overstuffed brown pillows, the pipestems of their legs, the blackened sneakers. He's inadvertently closed his good eye, the one that sees up close, and he has to go binocular—and risk a perilous moment of night-blindness—to read what it says on the bag.

King Kon-Crete, it reads, over the picture of a cartoon ape in sunglasses strutting around a wheelbarrow, *Premium Concrete. Mix Entire Bag with Water to Desired Consistency. Keep Away From Children.*

"Back to consistency again," Teo says, shuffling his feet round the bag, and that's all that can be seen of him, his feet—his diminutive feet, feet no bigger than Sierra's—in the cone of light descending from Andrea's hand. Tierwater can picture him, though, squat and muscular, his upper body honed from pumping iron and driving his longboard through the surf, his face delicate, his wrists and ankles tapered like a girl's. He's

20

so small and pumped he could be a special breed, a kind of human terrier, fearless, indefatigable, tenacious, and with a bark like—but enough. They need him here. They need him to say, "Shit, let's just dump the stuff and get it over with."

And so they do. They slit the bags and let the dependable force of gravity empty them. They haul the water in a thickening miasma of mosquitoes, swatting, cursing, unceremoniously upending the buckets atop the dry concrete. And then they mix and slice and chivvy till the trench is uniformly filled with something like cold lava, and the hour is finally at hand. "Ready, everybody?" Tierwater whispers. "Teo on the outside, Andrea next to Teo—and Sierra, you get in between me and Andrea, okay?"

"Aren't you forgetting something?" This is Andrea, exhausted, but reclaiming the initiative.

He looks round him in the dark, a wasted gesture. "No, what?"

A slight lilt to the tone, an edge of satisfaction. She's done her homework, she's seen the movie, memorized the poem, got in touch with her inner self. She has the information, and he doesn't. "The essential final step, the issue you've been avoiding all week except when you accused me of forgetting it—*them*, I mean?"

Then it hits him. "The diapers?"

Eighteen per package, at $16.99. They've had to invest in three different sizes—small, medium and large, for Sierra, Andrea and Teo, and himself, respectively—though Andrea assures him they'll use them up during the next direct action, whenever and wherever that may be. Either that, or give them away to volunteers. They're called, comfortingly enough, *Depends*, and on her advice they've chosen the Fitted Briefs for Extra Absorbency. He can't help thinking about that for just the smallest slice of a moment—*Extra Absorbency*—and about what it is the diapers are meant to absorb.

There's a moment of silence there in the dark, the naked woods crepitating round them, the alertest of the birds already calling out for dawn, when they're all communally involved in a very private act. The sound of zippers, the hopping on one foot, arms jerked out for balance, and then they're diapered and the jeans rise back up their legs to grab at their bellies and buttocks. He hasn't worn diapers—or pads, as the professionals euphemistically call them so as not to offend the Alzheimer's patients and other walking disasters who have to be swathed in them day and night—since he was an infant, and he doesn't remember much of that. He remembers Sierra, though, mewling and gurgling, kicking her shit-besmeared legs in the air, as he bent to the task on those rare occasions when her mother, who performed her role perfectly, was either absent or unconscious. They feel—not so bad, not yet anyway. Like underwear, like briefs, only thicker.

And now, finally, the time has come to compete the ritual and settle down to slap mosquitoes, slumber fitfully and await the first astonished Freddies (Forest Service types) and heavy machine operators. They join hands for balance, sink their cheap tennis sneakers into the wet concrete as deep as they'll go, and then ease themselves down on the tapered bottoms of their upended buckets. He will be miserable. His head will droop, his back will scream. He will bait mosquitoes and crap in his pants. But it's nothing. The smallest thing, the sacrifice of one night in bed with a book or narcotized in front of the tube—that, and a few hours of physical discomfort. And as he settles in, the concrete gripping his ankles like a dark set of jaws, the stars receding into the skullcap of the silvering sky and every bird alive in every tree, he tells himself *Somebody's got to do it.*

He must have dozed. He did doze—or sleep, would be more accurate. He slumped over his knees, put his head to rest and drifted into unconsciousness, because there was no sense in doing anything else, no matter his dreads and fears—nothing was going to happen till seven-thirty or eight at the earliest, and he put all that out of his mind and orchestrated his dreams to revolve around a man in bed, a man like him, thin as grass but big across the shoulders, with no gut or rear end to speak of and the first tentative fingers of hair loss massaging his skull, a man in an air-conditioned room in blissful deep non-REM sleep with something like Respighi's "The Birds" playing softly in the background.

And what does he wake to? Is it the coughing wheeze of a poorly tuned pickup beating along the road, the single mocking laugh of a raven, the low-threshold tocsin of his daughter's voice, soft and supple and caught deep in her throat, saying, "Uh . . . Dad. Dad, wake up?" Whatever it is, it jerks him up off the narrow stool of the bucket in one explosive motion, like a diver surging up out of the deepest pool, and he tries to lift his feet, to leap, to run, to escape the hammering in his chest. But his feet are locked in place. And his body, his upper body, is suddenly floundering forward without support, even as the image of the burnt-orange pickup with its grinning bumper and the swept-back mask of the glassed-in cab comes hurtling down the road toward him, toward *them* . . . but the knee joint isn't designed to give in that direction, and even in the moment of crisis—*Jesus Christ, the shithead's going to hit us!*—he lurches back and sits heavily and ignominiously on the bucket that even now is squirting out from under him. "Stop!" He roars, "Stop!" against a background of shrieks and protests, and somehow he's on his feet again and reaching out to his left, for his daughter, to pull her to him and cradle her against the moment of impact . . . Which, mercifully, never comes.

He wouldn't want to talk about the diapers, not in this context. He'd want to address the issue of the three intensely bearded, red-suspendered timber people wedged into the cab of that pickup, that scorching orange Toyota 4x4 that comes to rest in a demon-driven cloud of dust no more than ten feet from them. And the looks on their faces—their seven-thirty-in-the-a.m. faces, Egg McMuffins still warm in their bellies, searing coffee sloshed in their laps, the bills of their caps askew and their eyes crawling across their faces like slugs. This is the look of pure, otherworldly astonishment. (*Don't blame these men—or not yet, anyway. They didn't expect us to be there— they didn't expect anything, other than maybe a tardy coyote or a suicidal ground squirrel—and suddenly there we were, like some manifestation of the divine, like the lame made to walk and the blind to see.*)

"Oh, God," Andrea murmurs, and it's as if the air has been squeezed out of her lungs, and they're all standing now, erect and trembling and holding hands for lack of anything better to do. Tierwater cuts a swift glance from the stalled pickup to the face of his daughter. It's a tiny little dollop of a face, shrunken and drawn in on itself, the face of the little girl awake with the terror of the night and the scratchy voice and the need for reason and comprehension and the whispered assurance that the world into which she's awakened is the ancient one, the imperturbable one, the one that will go on twisting round its axis whether we're here to spin it or not. That face paralyzes him. What are they thinking? What are they doing?

"Christ Jesus, what is goin' on here?" comes the voice of the pickup, the unanimous voice, concentrated in the form of the pony-tailed and ginger-bearded head poking through the open window of the wide-swinging driver's side door. "You people lost or what?" A moment later, the rest of the speaker emerges, workboots, rolled-up jeans, a flannel shirt in some bleached-out shade of tartan plaid. His face is like an electric skillet. Like a fuse in the moment of burning out. "What in Christ's name is wrong with you? I almost—you know, I could of—" He's trembling too, his hands so shaky he has to bury them in his pockets.

Tierwater has to remind himself that this man—thirty-five, flat dead alcoholic eyes, the annealed imprint of a scar like a brand stamped into the flange of his nose—is not the enemy.

He's just earning his paycheck, felling and loading and producing so many board feet a year so middle-class Americans can exercise their God-given right to panel their family rooms and cobble together redwood picnic tables from incomprehensible sets of plans. He's never heard of Arne Naess or Deep Ecology or the mycorrhizal fungi that cling to the roots of old growth trees and make the forest possible. Rush Limbaugh wrote his bible, and the exegesis of it too. He has a T-shirt in a drawer at home that depicts a spotted owl in a frying pan. He knows incontrovertibly and with a kind of unconquerable serenity that all members of the Sierra Club are "Green Niggers" and that Earth Forever! is a front for Bolshevik terrorists with homosexual tendencies. But he's not the enemy. His bosses are.

"We're not letting you through," Teo announces, and there he is, a plug of muscle hammered into the ground, anchoring the far end of the human chain. All he needs is a slab of liver.

The other two have squeezed out of the truck by now, work-hardened men, incongruously bellied, looks of utter stupefaction on their faces. They just stare.

"What are you," the first man wants to know, the driver, the one in faded tartan, "environmentalists or something?" He's seen housewives, ministers, schoolchildren, drug addicts, drunks, ex-cons, jockeys, ballplayers, maybe even sexual deviates, but you can tell by the faltering interrogatory lift of the question that he's never in his life been face-to-face with the devil before.

"That's right," Tierwater says, radicalized already, gone from suburban drudge to outside agitator in eight months' time, "and you ought to be one too, if you want to keep your job beyond next year or even next month." He glances up at the palisade of the trees, needles stitched together like a quilt, the sun stalking through crowns and snags in its slow progress across the sky, and then he's confronting those blunted eyes again. And this is the strange part: he's not in bed dreaming, but actually standing in the middle of a concrete trench in a road in the middle of nowhere, wearing diapers and giving a speech—at seven-thirty in the morning, no less.

"What are you going to cut when all the trees are gone? You think your bosses care about that? You think the junk bond kings and the rest of the suits in New York give the slightest damn about you or your children or the mills or the trees or anything else?"

"Or retirement," Teo puts in. "What about retirement? Huh? I can't hear you. Talk to me. Talk to me, man, come on: *talk to me.*"

He isn't one for debate, this man, or consorting with environmentalists either. For a long moment he just stands there staring at them—at Tierwater, at Sierra, Andrea, Teo, at their linked hands and the alien strip of concrete holding them fast at the ankles. "Piss on you," he says finally, and in a concerted move he and his companions roll back into the pickup and the engine fires up with a roar. A screech of tires and fanbelt, and then he's reversing gears, jerking round and charging back down the road in the direction he came from. They're left with dust. With the mosquitoes. And the sun, which has just begun to slash through the trees and make its first radiant impression

27

on their faces and hands and the flat black cotton and polyester that clothe them.

"I'm hungry. I'm tired. I want to go home."

His daughter is propped up on her bucket, limp as an invertebrate, and she's trying to be brave, trying to be an adult, trying to prove she's as capable of manning the barricades as anybody, but it isn't working. The sun is already hot, though it's just past ten by Tierwater's watch, and they've long since shed their sweatshirts. They've kept the caps on, for protection against the sun, and they've referred to their water bags and consumed the sandwiches Andrea so providentially brought along, and what they're doing now is waiting. Waiting for the confrontation, the climax, the reporters and TV cameras, the sheriff and his deputies. Tierwater can picture the jail cell, cool shadows playing off the walls, the sound of a flushing toilet, a cot to stretch out on. They'll have just long enough to close their eyes, no fears, no problems, events leaping on ahead of them—bailed out before the afternoon is over, the EF! lawyers on alert, everything in place. Everything but the sheriff, that is. What could be keeping him?

"How much longer, Andrea? Really. Because I want to know, and don't try to patronize me either."

He wants to say, *It's all right, baby, it'll be over soon,* but he's not much good at comforting people, even his own daughter—Bear up, that's his philosophy. Tough it out. Think of the Mohawk, whose captives had to laugh in the face of the knife, applaud their own systematic dismemberment, cry out in mirth as their skin came away in bloody tapering strips. He leaves it to Andrea, who coos encouragement in a voice that's like a salve. Numbed, he watches her reach out to exchange Sierra's vampire novel (which, under the circumstances, hasn't proved lurid enough) for a book of crossword puzzles.

Teo, at the opposite end of the line, is a model of stoicism. Hunched over the upended bucket like a man perched on the throne in the privacy of his own bathroom, his eyes roaming the trees for a glimpse of wildlife instead of scanning headlines in the paper, he's utterly at home, unperturbed, perfectly willing to accept the role of martyr, if that's what comes to him. Tierwater isn't in his league, and he'd be the first to admit it. His feet itch, for one thing—a compelling, imperative itch that brings tears to his eyes—and the concrete, still imperceptibly hardening, has begun to chew at his ankles beneath the armor of his double socks and stiffened jeans. He has a full-blown headache too, the kind that starts behind the eyes and works its way through the cortex to the occipital lobe and back again in pulses as rhythmic and regular as waves beating against the shore. He has to urinate. Even worse, he can feel a bowel movement coming on.

Another hour oozes by. He's been trying to read—Bill McKibben's *The End of Nature*—but his eyes are burning and the relentless march of premonitory rhetoric makes him suicidal. Or maybe homicidal. It's hot. Very hot. Unseasonably hot. And though they're all backpackers, all four of them, exposed regularly to the sun, this is something else altogether, this is like some kind of torture—like the sweat box in *The*

Bridge on the River Kwai—and when he lifts the bota bag to his lips for the hundredth time, Andrea reminds him to conserve water. "The way it's looking," she says, and here is the voice of experience, delivered with a certain grim satisfaction, "we could be here a long time yet."

And then, far off in the distance, a sound so attenuated they can't be sure they've heard it. It's the sound of an internal combustion engine, a diesel, blat-blatting in the interstices between dips in the road. The noise grows louder, they can see the poisoned billows of black exhaust, and all at once a bulldozer heaves into view, scuffed yellow paint, treads like millwheels, and the bulbous face of determination and outrage at the controls. The driver lumbers straight for them, as if he's blind, the shovel lowered to reap the standing crop of them, to shear them off at the ankles like a row of dried-out cornstalks. Tierwater is on his feet suddenly, on his feet again, reaching out instinctively for his daughter's hand, and "Dad," she's saying, "does he know? Does he know we can't move?"

It's the pickup truck all over again, only worse: the four of them shouting till the veins stand out in their necks, Andrea and Teo waving their arms over their heads, the sweat of fear and mortal tension prickling at their scalps and private places, and that's exactly what the man on the Cat wants. He knows perfectly well what's going on here—they all do by now, from the supervisors down to the surveying crews, and his object is intimidation, pure and simple. All those gleaming pumping tons of steel in motion, the big tractor treads burning up the road and the noise of the thing, still coming at them at full speed, and Tierwater can't see the eyes of the lunatic at the controls—*shades, he's wearing mirror shades that give him an evil insectoid look, no mercy, no appeal*—and suddenly he's outraged, ready to kill: this is one sick game. At the last conceivable moment, a raw-knuckled hand jerks back a lever and the thing rears like a horse and swivels away from them with a kind of mechanized grace he wouldn't have believed possible.

But that's only the first pass, and it carries the bulldozer into the wall of rock beside them with a concussive blast, sparks spewing from the blade, the shriek of one unyielding surface meeting another, and Tierwater can feel the crush of it in his feet, even as the shards of stone and dirt rain down on him. He's no stranger to violence. His father purveyed it, his mother suffered it, his first wife died of it—the most casual violence in the world, in a place as wild as this. He's new at pacifism or masochism or whatever you'd want to call what they're suffering here, and if he could free his legs for just half a minute, he'd drag that tight-jawed executioner down off his perch and instruct him in the laws of the flesh, he would. But he can't do a thing. He's caught. Stuck fast in the glue of passive resistance, Saint Mahatma and Rosa Parks and James Meredith flashing through his mind in quick review. And he's swearing to himself *Never again, never,* even as the man with the stick and eight tons of screaming iron and steel swings round for the second pass, and then the third and the fourth.

But that's enough. That's enough right there. Tyrone Tierwater wouldn't want to remember what that did to his daughter or the look on her face or the sad sick feeling of his

31

own impotence. The sheriff came, with two deputies, and he took his own sweet time about it. And what did he do when he finally did get there? Did he arrest the man on the Cat? Close down the whole operation and let the courts decide if it's legal to bulldoze a dead zone through a federally designated roadless area? No. He handcuffed the four of them—even Sierra—and his deputies had a good laugh ripping the watch-caps off their heads, wadding them up and flinging them into the creek, and they caught a glimpse of the curtains parting on redneck heaven when they cut the straps of the bota bags and flung them after the hats. And then, for good measure, smirking all the while, these same deputies got a nice little frisson out of kicking the buckets out from under Tierwater and his wife and daughter and good friend, one at a time, and then settling in to watch them wait three interminable hours in the sun for the men with the sledgehammers.

Andrea cursed the deputies, and they cursed her back. Teo glared from the cave of his muscles. Tierwater was beside himself. He raged and bellowed and threatened them with everything from aggravated assault to monetary damages and prosecution for police brutality—at least until the sheriff, Sheriff Bob Hicks of Josephine County, produced a roll of duct tape and shut his mouth for him. And his daughter, his tough, right-thinking, long-haired, tree-hugging, animal-loving, vege-tarian daughter—she folded herself up like an umbrella over the prison of her feet and cried. Thirteen years old, tired, scared, and she just let herself go. (*They shuffled their workboots and looked shamefaced then, those standard-issue badge-polishers*

32

and the Forest Service officials who drove up in a green Jeep to join them—they probably had daughters themselves, and sons and dogs and rabbits in a hutch—but there was nothing any of them could do about my little girl's grief. Least of all me.)

Grateful for a day's reprieve, the Pacific salamanders curled up under the cover of their rocks, the martens retreated into the canopy and the spotted owls winked open an eye at the sound of that thin disconsolate wail of human distress. Tierwater's hands were bound, his mouth taped. Every snuffle, every choked-back sob, was a spike driven into the back of his head.

Yes. And here's the irony, the kicker, the sad, deflating and piss-poor denouement. For all they went through that morning, for all the pain and boredom and humiliation, there wasn't a single reporter on hand to bear witness, because Sheriff Bob Hicks had blocked the road at the highway and wouldn't let anyone in—and so it was a joke, a big joke, the whole thing. He can remember sitting there frying like somebody's meal with a face, no ozone layer left to protect them from the sun, no water, no hat and no shade and all the trees of the world under the axe, while he worked out the conundrum in his head: If a protest falls in the woods and there's no one there to hear it, does it make a sound?

ZOOGOING

by Lydia Millet

The zoo was on the edge of a wide desert valley, with a view of cactus-dotted hills above and, in the flats spread out beneath, flocks of small white houses. He went there after a meeting in Scottsdale, to fill an empty afternoon. He was restless in his hotel and had seen the zoo in a tourist brochure, with a picture of a wolf.

In a series of arid gardens connected by pathways there was a hummingbird enclosure and an aviary, a beaver pond and a pool for otters; there were Mexican parrots squawking, bighorn sheep on artificial cliffs, an ocelot curled up in a rocky crevice and a sleek bobcat pacing restlessly. He passed a lush pollinator garden and a series of low and inconspicuous buildings; an elderly, white-haired docent stood with a watchful bird perched on her hand, waiting for interest. He wandered over and looked at the bird closely. It had large eyes in a beautiful face, and was compact but fierce looking.

"American kestrel," said the docent. "One of the smaller raptors. This gal is almost nine inches long, but weighs less than four ounces. Beautiful, isn't she?"

A few minutes later he stood bracing himself with his hands on a low wall over a moat. Across the moat slept a black bear on a sunny ledge. This was a zoo of animals native to the region, and though bears did not live in the hot flatlands a handful of them still roamed the piney mountains that rose above the desert floor. He had read that every so often a bear was found dead atop a power pole, where it had climbed suddenly in terror, escaping from a car or a noise, and been electrocuted.

He watched the bear sleep, and in the lull of the sun and the heat and the stillness felt like dozing off himself.

Then the stillness was disturbed by yelling boys, hitting each other in the face. The father, in shorts, stood at T.'s elbow, looking down into his camera and adjusting a ring on the lens. A projectile—someone had lobbed a balled-up piece of litter. It hit the bear a glancing blow on the ear and he stirred, disoriented, turned around once and then settled down again.

"Too soon, I wasn't set up yet. Missed the shot," said the man, shaking his head. "Go again."

The wife looked around for something else to throw and T. felt heat filling his face. A tension bowed in him: he felt a rush of fury.

"Are you kidding?" he asked, turning to the wife. She wore large mirrored sunglasses. "You're throwing garbage at the bear? For a *picture*?"

"What's the big deal?" said the family man.

36

"Don't do it," said T. His shoulders were fluid and nervy, his face shining. He was enraged. Or excited. But all here, he thought: and *I will kill them.* Even though he knew it was a posture, he felt the anger and relished it.

The man shrugged and the wife began rifling through her purse, apparently ignoring him; a few feet away one of the flailing children, a thin boy in khaki camouflage pants, was already lofting a second missile, a foam cup half-full of brown slush. The cup missed the bear and fell into the moat below, and the slush slung out of the cup as it arced past and dimpled the bear's dark coat. The bear reared up again, doubly confused.

The thin boy jeered.

T. turned to the father, who was still fumbling with his zoom lens. A split second of hesitation. "You let your kid do that again, I swear to God I'll grab that camera and break it open on the cement," he said.

He realized his molars were grinding. He had never done this, never. Never anything—. He was thrilled and at the same time he hated the man, hated his wife and even his children.

"Mind your own business," said the family man.

"I'm dead serious. I'll smash it to fucking bits."

"I'll sue you!"

"What are you thinking? Seriously. What does someone like you think? Do you think?"

"Stupid bear!" jeered the camouflage kid.

"Mind your business," said the family man again.

"It *is* my business," said T. "Just like it would be if you threw

37

garbage at my sister. What don't you get about that? Is there an argument for what you're doing?"

"Let's just go, Ray," said the wife.

"I got a squirt gun," said the kid, and pulled it out: the size of an assault rifle, bright pink.

"Don't even think about it," said T., and looked at the father. His neck tensed, his hands flexed. "Tell him to put that thing away. I'll punch your face. I mean it."

The man was squaring off, his eyes narrowed. He let his camera rest against his chest, the dangling lens cap swinging.

"Tell *me* how to handle my kid? He can squirt his water gun at the bear if he wants to."

"You disgusting. Piece. Of shit," said T.

The wife tugged urgently on her husband's sleeve.

"Come *on*, Ray."

After a moment the family man turned, his wife beside him and the kids ranging around them both; as they turned a corner the kid in camouflage pants whipped around and sneered, sticking up the middle fingers of both hands before he disappeared.

T. felt the adrenaline surge fade but still he burned. He wanted to hunt them down and punish them. But he did not. He did not utter a word of complaint to the zoo's management. He was flooded with elation.

He was elated. This was who he was, he thought; he was a person who would defend, who would swear and threaten and feel the heat and the cliff-edge of opinion. He felt good—better than good. He stood there for seconds, or was it forever?—stood there partway in rapture, struck.

Zoogoing

On its flat rock the bear was still turning blearily round, tossing its head as though trapped in a nightmare. Finally it resettled itself and laid its chin on its paws to go back to sleep.

He went back that night when the zoo was closed, thrilled, as if he was lightly drunk, at the illicitness in himself. It was new. What arrested him in the zoo was the wildness it contained—how far this was from the realm of his competence. He wanted to meet it. He knew the zoo animals lived in cages but nothing more about them except that they were alone, most of them, not only alone in the cages, often, but alone on the earth, vanishing. Their condition was close to what he was trying to grasp, lay somehow at the base of his growing suspicion that the ground was no longer fixed, was shifting beneath him.

Empire only looked good built against a backdrop of oceans and forests. It needed them. If the oceans were dead and the forests replaced by pavement even empire would be robbed of its consequence. *Alone*, he thought—a word that came to him more and more, in singsong like a jeer. In the zoo the rare animals might have been orphaned or captured or even born in captivity. He had no idea where they came from, could not know their individual histories. But he knew their position, as he knew his own: they were at the forefront of aloneness, like pioneers. They were the ones sent ahead to see what the new world was like.

Would they tell what they saw?

The rarest animal in the zoo was a Mexican gray wolf, the one pictured in the tourist brochure, an animal that was apparently frail and aging. Its fur looked mangy; it had been asleep when he was there earlier. The wolf's pen, as the sign posted on it told him, was a temporary setup during construction of a new exhibit. It was nothing more substantial than a chain-link fence near the road, with barbed wire curling along the top.

He looked at his shoes: round toes. He should be able to wedge them into the holes. He shoved his flashlight in his pocket, hooked his fingers through the mesh and pulled himself up, kicking for purchase. His feet flailed against the fencing and his fingers were already bruising, imprinted with purple lines. Speed was the key, he thought, move quickly. He always had reasons for each single action, but he had no good reasons for doing this. Was he irrational? But it lifted him. He would follow the question to its resolution, even if the question was unconscious.

He was not even all the way up the six-foot fence when he regretted his tactics. He had to get down from here, the pressure on the pads of his fingertips, which he feared were going to be sliced clean through. In a scramble he grabbed the metal frame the wire was stretched on and went up and over it, catching barbs on his chest and thighs. His leg, halfway over, was tangled in the wire, and struggling he lost his foothold. Falling he tried to launch himself forward, away from the barbs.

When he recovered, on the ground with an aching neck and shoulders, he had a sharp pain in his leg. Sitting up he saw he had grazed his calf on a cactus as he fell. Through the thin cotton of his pants it was bleeding, and in the dark he could see white spines sticking through the fabric. He stood unsteadily, bracing himself against the fence; he could make out almost nothing. He walked around the cactus, lifting his flashlight. In the dark he could imagine not only wolves but almost anything, a secret menagerie. He was filled with the rush of this, with the idea of myriad creatures materializing from the blackness. Their coats glowed, their faces were both benign and predatory. The faces of animals were amazing in that, tongues of velvet and claws of ice. What were they?

There was a gate, padlocked; a metal box built into the base of the fence; a dry log, a thin tree. Doves rose suddenly from the tree, a flurry of hysterical wingbeats. He jumped.

His leg was aching.

He began to point his beam at bushes and the bases of trees, where holes might be tucked. Finally he flicked off the light and squatted down. Without the glare his eyes adjusted and finally he apprehended a shape that was not a bush or tree, hunkered down against the fence, low and dim.

He got up silently and picked his way closer, still without the flashlight on, his eyes on the ground while he threaded his way between bushes. Closer and closer till he pointed the flashlight toward the ground in front of the wolf's hunched shape and touched the switch with his thumb. A quick yellow flicker of eyes and then the wolf moved fluidly, fleeing along the fence. It went away from him, into a corner where it remained.

He would not get closer. The wolf would not allow it.

✻   ✻   ✻

The next morning he removed the small spines from his leg. The wound was throbbing, but he did not mind; there was something he savored in it, pinching the hair-thin fibers hard between the tweezer edges. The sensation was fine and sharp as a grass blade. It satisfied him.

He took two aspirins and showered. In his socks and his shirt, standing in front of the in-room coffeemaker, he thought of the old wolf again. Animals were self-contained and people seemed to hold this against them—possibly because most of them had come to believe that animals should be like servants or children. Either they should work for men, suffer under a burden, or they should entertain them. He had strained against the wolf's aloofness himself, resenting the wolf for its insistence on distance. He had felt it almost as an insult, and inwardly he retaliated.

But then he was self-contained too: he had a private purpose, a trajectory, and no one had license to block it. It might be obscure even to him, but that obscurity was his own possession. The old wolf's unwillingness to be near him was fully forgiven by the light of day and in fact the joke was on him. Wariness was simply its way of life, having nothing to do with him. It had not been robbed of this quality, though it was caged and it was solitary: it retained its essence. It did not attempt to ingratiate itself. It did not have diplomacy.

He thought he recalled feeling, in the flash of its eyeshine, a similar flash in himself—a fleeting awareness that in the wolf's gaze there was a directness unlike the directness of men.

Wolves were gone, the educational sign on the cage had read, from most of the country. They were the villains of fairy tales, and there had been vast campaigns to exterminate them all across the continent. A slaughter of the wolves, along with the buffalo. Long before that in the late Pleistocene, according to the sign, the Clovis people had caused the extinction of the cave bear, the giant beaver, the saber-tooth tiger, the horse and the mastodon.

He buttoned his shirt without looking at his fingers, eyes on a weather map on the television, a smiling weatherman pointing and gesturing. He had wanted the old wolf to come close to him, head down, softening. As though all wild animals could one day be tamed—as though this was an aspect of all of them, this one-day-tamable quality, and their wildness was nothing more than coyness or a mannerism. As though other animals should not only submit to people but behave like them, comport themselves with civility.

Privately, he thought, at the heart of it, you wanted animals to turn to you in welcome. It was a habit gained from expecting each other to do this, from expecting this of other people and only knowing people, not knowing anything beyond them. That was another kind of solitude, the kind where there was nothing all around but reflections.

And what about the endless differences of the animals, their strange bodies? Many legs, stripes, a fiery orangeness; curved teeth or tentacles, wings or scales or sky-blue eggs . . . instead of looking at the wolf as an animal he never knew and never could, as with the sacred and the divine, he had fallen into the trap. He had wanted it to lick his hand and lope along beside him.

✳   ✳   ✳

The animals were very busy with dying, not only one at a time but in sweeps and categories. This he found increasingly distressing. He began to comb newspapers for the latest word about animals vanishing; he began subscribing to magazines. In magazine pictures he saw animals far away, in the places where they had been born and either continued to live or began to die off. Some were in backgrounds of green, others yellow, others a bright turquoise. White now and then, Siberia or the Antarctic. These were the places of the animals' origin, warm green, dry yellow, the wet deep blue.

Then there was the gray of human habitation. The blue places were turning to brown, the yellow places to dust, the green places to smoke and ashes. Each time one of the animals disappeared—they went by species or sometimes by organizations of species, interconnected—it was as though all mountains were gone, or all lakes. A certain form of the world. But in the gray that metastasized over continents and hemispheres few appeared to be deterred by this extinguishing or even to speak of it, no one outside fringe elements and elite groups, professors and hippies, small populations of little general importance. The quiet mass disappearance, the inversion of the Ark, was passing unnoticed; on this hot globe, a third of all species would soon be gone. The flocks of passenger pigeons that had once darkened the sky, Teddy Roosevelt on safari shooting hundreds of animals from a train . . . he saw a list from one of Roosevelt's trips to Africa in 1909. Five hundred and twelve animals shot, including seventeen lions, eleven elephants, twenty rhinos, nine giraffes, forty-seven gazelles, eight hippos, and twenty-nine zebras. George V of England had killed a thousand birds in one day for sport; in a year the Roman emperor Titus had nine thousand captured animals killed in popular displays.

He soon learned to recognize the signs of an animal's imminent disappearance. Some were tagged or collared or photographed, some monitored by bureaucrats. Sometimes a group or individual took up the cause of an animal or a plant and could muster the rationale for a lawsuit, and often the courts favored the victim; but the victim remained a victim and for each victim whose passing was noted thousands more slid away in the dark. From where he stood they succumbed with great ease; from where he stood they had always been invisible anyway.

Animals in the outside were far from his life, but zoos were close at hand. Zoos would be his study.

His practical lessons took place at nighttime, which left his days free for commerce. At first he read mail-order manuals but soon they left him at loose ends and he hired a locksmith to teach him. The locksmith, a Brazilian, came to his apartment twice a week and brought his full toolkit: hooks, rakes, diamonds, balls, tension wrenches. They practiced on T.'s doors and cabinets, on a variety of locks the locksmith installed for the purpose.

After the lesson the locksmith would often stay for a nightcap; T. had assured him that he would not use his hard-won knowledge to commit crimes against persons or property, and though he had the impression the locksmith could not care less whether he used his powers for good or for ill the friendly assurances served as a bridge between them. Criminal trespass would be the limit, he said jokily. The Brazilian stayed to drink with him on Fridays and sometimes played a few hands of cards.

His nights were not always free, however. He was still not delivered of Fulton, his investor, despite the fact that he had professed bursitis to get out of playing racquetball; Fulton's wife had taken him under her wing. As a young man with no clear defects or blemishes, with his health and his wealth and a full head of hair, he was apparently eligible and became an object of desire for many women newly introduced to him.

It was Janet's calling to bring him and these wanting women together. Janet did not believe it was feasible to be single; to Janet a bachelor eked out his living on the margins of society, orbiting the married couples wild-eyed and feral as a homeless man at a polo party. A single man, to Janet, was superior in the social hierarchy only to a single woman—this last a life form that was repellent but fortunately short-lived, naked and glistening as it gobbled its way out of its larval cocoon.

Because Fulton was an investor T. could not refuse his hospitality on every occasion, and so at least once a week he found himself a dinner guest at Fulton's house in Brentwood. It was an article of faith with Janet that when men brought wealth to the table women must bring good looks; and since this was Los Angeles there was always someone sitting across from him—not too much older than he, for Janet had imposed a limit of thirty to allow time for courtship, engagement, and a brief honeymoon followed by reproduction—whose hair had been bleached, breasts lifted, or nose pinched into narrowness above delicately flared nostrils.

Janet was a homemaker by choice, a Texas debutante whose father had gifted her with a dowry that had made her attractive to a legion of Fultons; what distinguished her own Fulton was chiefly that he had beaten other suitors to the punch. So the women she brought to meet T. were seldom burdened by such useless accessories as an academic record or a sense of social purpose. They tended to be certain of their attractiveness and accustomed to admiration; they were eager to begin a conversation with him but not always sure where to take it. One of them asked him what he did for a living and then, after he told her, smiled, twirled her hair around a finger and gazed at him glassily, as though fully expecting him to run with the discussion from that point onward.

At first he tried to be polite to show deference to Janet, but as the dinners wore on over the weeks he saw he had to discourage the women, smoothly and cannily, without allowing them to say precisely what it was in his manner that had pushed them away. Janet should see only that the women, despite their initial surge of interest, would never quite warm to him.

He applied himself thus to the task of quiet repulsion; and as he grew competent at lock-picking the pace of Janet's dinner invitations began finally to slacken.

"I don't know what your problem is, man," said Fulton as he was leaving one night, following an encounter with an interior decorator named Ligi who had wished to talk only of upholstery. "Why don't you make a move for once?"

"Listen, Janet needs to stop setting me up," said T. gently. "I appreciate her good intentions. But I'm not in the market."

"Jesus, you don't have to *marry* them," said Fulton. "But they're better than K/Y and Carpal Tunnel."

"Not to me," said T.

"That's hardcore," said Fulton.

In New York for a business meeting he drove to the Bronx at night. The lock was easy. A low metal gate in a grove of thin trees, then a walk across a dark, wide square. Lights reflected on a sea-lion pool.

On the second lock his fingers slipped nervously, but soon he was in. His neck was wet and his heart rate rapid; he heard the rush of blood in his ears. He slipped the tools back into his pack, stood still and made himself slow his breathing. He had read a zoo press release. "The most endangered mammal in the world, the Sumatran rhinoceros has not bred in captivity since 1889." Penlight beam focused, he read the card: *Dicerorhinus sumatrensis*. It was the only one in captivity in the United States and it was a dinosaur; its species had lived for fifteen million years and there were only a few hundred left. A female.

She hauled herself up as he stood there, hauled herself up and walked a few steps away. She was nosing hay or straw, whatever dry grass littered the floor of her room. She gave an impression of oblong brownness. The Sumatran rhinoceros, he had read, liked mud wallows. Here there was nothing but floor.

He was standing where any zoo patron could stand, and there was no danger or special privilege. Still, no one was around—he was alone with her—and he was content. It was not to claim the animal's attention that he was here but to let her claim his. She was the only one of her kind for thousands of miles, across the wide seas. What person had ever known such separation?

The Sumatran rhinoceros reportedly had a song, difficult for the human ear to follow; its song had been mapped and similarities had been found between this song and the song of the humpback whale. It was not singing now.

Sight was less important to a rhinoceros than to him, he knew that, but she still had to see. He put his hand to his nose, blocking sight between his own two eyes, closing one and then the other. He had read that the vision of many animals was dichromatic; they saw everything in a scheme based on two primary colors, not three. Were they red, he thought, red and blue? He closed his own eyes, heard the rise and fall of his chest and nearby a rustle whose nature he could not discern. Behind the eyelids it was thick and dark but impressions of light passed there, distracting. They passed like clouds he found himself idly drawn to interpret, to fix into the shape of rabbits or swans.

After a while the rhinoceros sighed. It was a familiar sound despite the fact that they were strangers. He knew the need for the sigh, the feel of its passage; a sigh was not a thought but substituted for one, a sign of grief or affection, of putting down something heavy that was carried too long. In the wake of the sigh he wondered exactly how lonely she was, in this minute that held the two of them. Maybe she saw beyond herself, the future after she had disappeared; maybe she had an instinct for the meaning of boundaries and closed doors, of the conditions of her captivity or the terminus of her line, hers and her ancestors'.

Maybe she had no idea.

He put a hand against the cool wall and felt almost leaden. No other animal could have eyes shaped like these, see the ground and the trees from this place with this dinosaur's consciousness. No other hide would feel the warmth of the sun wash over these molecules, and neither he nor anyone would know how it had felt to live there, in both the particulars and the generalities, the sad quiescence of the animal's own end of time.

He never spoke of his incursions and guarded carefully the difference between himself and the self that was available publicly. This was a clear benefit of being alone. A partner would have broken the seal.

With meticulous care he planned his business trips in relation to sanctuaries and captive breeding facilities, finding reasons to fly to these places even when profit was unlikely. Undetected he entered a bird sanctuary in San Diego, a rescue center for manatees scarred by boat propellers, a butterfly habitat in New Hampshire, a laboratory in Rhode Island where American burying beetles were bred and released. He was a regular at the best zoos in California, Arizona and New Mexico and he also flew to others—St. Louis, Seattle, Cincinnati. Each night he reserved for a single enclosure.

And he took a course in basic first aid that stood him in good stead. His thighs stayed lightly scarred from the tree in the Monkey House, whose superficial but stinging cuts had proved slow to heal; his knees scabbed over from multiple abrasions he tended to reopen, and his right calf bore the purple marks of teeth from a young Morelet's crocodile. It had been a fairly fortunate encounter in fact—the baby crocodile had let go almost right away, allowing him to drag himself out of its pen sheepishly, hurting but mostly ashamed of his carelessness. The punctures were not deep and did not require stitches; he slathered them in antibiotic ointment and left it at that.

So that no one would notice the marks he ran his half-marathons in long pants; should anyone ask, he was rock climbing, in the mountains and at the gym. Thence came the battered kneecaps, the scrapes on his elbows and knuckles and cuts on his fingertips.

At the beginning he was afraid of the predators, and though he chose with great care, avoiding animals known to be highly territorial or prone to aggression, he was still wary. They were not pets. But he soon lost this novice fear. It was not his habit to stalk the animals, merely to enter their enclosures and sit in one place to observe them. So he waited for each animal to show itself, and over time he grew tired, then bored; he was amazed at the depth and reach of his boredom, the way minutes and hours wore on uneventfully. For the animals too the greater part of captivity was waiting: when their food was delivered the last animals fed, slept and briefly forgot, he believed, the urgency of hunger. Then they awoke and the waiting started again.

He wished he knew if they got impatient. Expectation struck him as a human impulse, but then he thought of his dog. Her days were entirely given over to expectation, it seemed to him.

Waiting for a feeding the animals paced or swam or leapt from branch to branch, as their natures dictated, with a bat now and then at a so-called enrichment tool or a peck at an errant insect. Their lives were simple monotony. They slept to use up time; this was how their days were spent, the last sons and daughters.

In the wild, he thought, there would be almost no waiting. Waiting was what happened to you when you lost control, when events were out of your hands or your freedom was taken from you; but in the wild there would always be trying. In the wild there must be trying and trying, he thought, and no waiting at all. Waiting was a position of dependency. Not that animals in the wild were not watchful, did not have to freeze in place, alert and unmoving—they must do so often—but it would hardly be waiting then. It would be more like pausing.

Time must run more quickly there, matching heat and cold to the light of day and the dark of night. Familiarity with this pace would spin out through long days, as though it would never change: now and then would come quick fear or a close call, but mostly the ease of doing what had always been done. For a second a prey animal might grow complacent, and then in a rush the end came. As the animal moved where it had always moved, a scent on the wind might stop it. The last surge of adrenaline, the lightheadedness of a bloodletting: sleep again in the fade, in the warm ground of home. And how different could it be when the death was a last death? Say an individual was the very last of its kind. Say it was small— one of the kangaroo rats for instance—and ran from a young fox through a hardscrabble field, towering clouds casting long shadows over the grass. The run lasted a few seconds only; no one was watching, no one at all because there was no one for miles around, no one but insects and worms and a jet passing high overhead. Say neither of them knew either, the fox or the rat, that the rat was the last, that no rat like him would ever be born again. Was it different then? Did the world feel the loss? The field stayed a field, the sky remained blue. Any pause that occurred as the action unfurled, any split-second shifting of the vast tableau would have to be imagined by an onlooker who did not exist. The fox started to run again, looking for his next quarry since the last animal had been barely a mouthful. And yet a particular way of existence was gone, a whole volume in the library of being. Others were sure to fall afterward— a long fly with iridescent wings that lived only in the nest of this single rat, say; a parasite that lived under the wing of the fly; a flowering plant whose roots were nourished by the larval phase of the parasite; a bat that pollinated the plant . . . it was time that would show the loss, only time that would show how the world had been stripped of its mysteries, stripped by the hundreds and thousands and millions. Remaining would be only the pigeons and the raccoons. But it was not the domino effect he considered most often, simply the state of being last. Loss was common, a loss like his own; he couldn't pretend to the animals' isolation, although he flattered himself that he could imagine it. One day, he knew, it would be men that were last. In the silence of the exhibits he thought he could feel time changing him too, atom by atom. He was so bored one night that he lost resistance to falling asleep. It would be good to let himself go, he decided: so he did.

After that sleep was part of the routine, and sleeping he surrendered—it was up to the animals what happened. He was not protected anymore by the city and its installations. Lying down in the exhibits with them, awkward, uncomfortable, and finally overcome; creeping out before the keepers appeared for the morning feeding. While he slept, as far as he knew, the animals did not mean to approach him. But when he woke up they were sometimes near him by happenstance. In this way he saw a ringtail nosing her young down into the entry of her den and a hyena tearing hungrily at the breast of a pigeon.

SACRED SPACE

by Kim Stanley Robinson

Every summer Charlie Quibler flew back to California to spend a week in the Sierra Nevada, backpacking with a group of old friends. Most of them knew each other from high school, and some of them had gone to UC San Diego together, many years before. That they and Charlie's D.C. friend Frank Vanderwal had been undergraduates at UCSD at the same time had come up at dinner one night at the Quiblers' the previous winter, causing a moment of surprise, then a shrug. Possibly they had been in classes together—they couldn't remember. The subject had been dropped, as just one of those coincidences that often cropped up in the capital; so many people came from somewhere else that sometimes the elsewheres were the same.

This coincidence, however, was certainly a factor in Charlie inviting Frank to join the group for this summer's trip. Perhaps it played a part in Frank's acceptance as well; it was hard for Charlie to tell. Frank's usual reticence had recently scaled new heights.

The invitation had been Anna's idea. Frank was having an operation on an area behind his nose, which he described as "No big deal." But Anna just shook her head at that; "It's right next to his brain," she told Charlie. Frank had recently changed jobs, and did not particularly like the move from the National Science Foundation to his advisory position at the White House, she felt, but he certainly worked very long hours there. She felt her former colleague led a lonely existence at a time when he needed support.

This was all news to Charlie, despite the kayaking expeditions the two men had been on together. Frank normally seemed unassailably independent, and it was always a shock to see a person one regarded as unemotional suddenly become distraught.

So, soon after Frank had the surgery they visited him in the hospital, and he said he was fine, that it had gone well, he had been told. And yes, he would like to join the backpacking trip, thanks. It would be good to get away. Would he be okay to go to high altitude? Charlie wondered. He said he would be.

After that everyone was busy, with summer daycamp and swim lessons for their eldest son, Nick, policy papers for Charlie, daycare for Joe, and NSF for Anna; and they did not see Frank again for a couple weeks, until suddenly the time for the Sierra trip was upon them.

Charlie's California friends were fine with the idea of adding a member to the trip, which they had done from time to time before, and they were looking forward to meeting him.

"He's kind of quiet," Charlie warned them.

*　　*　　*

This annual trek had been problematized for Charlie on the home front ever since Nick's birth, him being the stay-at-home parent; and Joe's arrival had made things more than twice as bad. Two consecutive summers had passed without Charlie being able to make the trip. Anna had seen how despondent he had gotten on the days when his friends were hiking in the high Sierra without him, and she was the one who had suggested he just make whatever kid coverage arrangement it would take, and go. Gratefully Charlie had jumped up and kissed her, and between some logistical help on the Nick summer day camp front from an old Gymboree friend, and extended daycare for Joe, he found they had coverage for both boys for the same several hours a day, which meant Anna could continue to work almost full-time. This was crucial; the loss of even a couple of hours of work a day caused her brow to furrow vertically and her mouth to set in a this-is-not-good expression very particular to work delays.

Charlie knew the look well, but tried not to see it as the departure time approached.

"This will be good for Frank," he would say. "That was a good idea you had."

"It'll be good for you too," Anna would reply; or not reply at all and just give him a look.

Actually she would have been completely fine with him going, Charlie thought, if it were not that she still seemed to have some residual worries about Joe's health. When Charlie realized this by hearing her make some non sequitur that skipped from the one subject to the other, he was surprised; he had thought he was the only one still worrying about Joe. He had assumed Anna would have had her mind put fully at ease by the disappearance of the fever. That had always been the focus of her concern, as opposed to the matters of mood and behavior which had been bothering Charlie.

Now, however, as the time for the mountain trip got closer and closer, he could see on Anna's face all her expressions of worry, visible in quick flashes when they discussed things, or when she was tired. Charlie could read a great deal on Anna's face; he didn't know if this was just the ordinary result of long familiarity or if she were particularly expressive, but certainly her worried looks were very nuanced, and, he had to say, beautiful. Perhaps it was just because they were so legible to him. You could see that life *meant something* when she was worrying over it; her thoughts flickered over her face like flames over burning coals, as if one were watching some dreamily fine silent screen actress, able to express anything with looks alone. To read her was to love her. She might be, as Charlie thought she was, slightly crazy about work, but even that was part of what he loved, as just another manifestation of how much she cared about things. One could not care more and remain sane. Mostly sane.

But Anna had never admitted, or even apparently seen, the connections Charlie had spotted between external events and the various changes in Joe. To her there was no such thing as a metaphysical illness, because there was no such thing as metaphysics. And there was no such thing as psychosomatic illness in a two-year-old, because a toddler was not old enough to have problems, as another Gymboree friend had put it.

So it had to be a fever. Or so she must have been subconsciously reasoning. Charlie had to intuit or deduce most of this from the kinds of apprehension he saw in her. He wondered what would happen if Anna were the one on hand when Joe went into one of his little trances. He wondered if she knew Joe's daytime behavior well enough to notice the myriad tiny shifts that had recently occurred in his daily moods.

Well, of course she did; but whether she would admit that some of these changes might indicate some special sensitivity in their son was another matter.

Maybe it was better that she couldn't be convinced. Charlie himself did not want to think there was anything real to this line of thought. It was one of his own forms of worry, perhaps—trying to find some explanation other than undiagnosed disease or mental problem. Even if the alternative explanation might in some ways be worse. Because it disturbed him, even occasionally freaked him out. He could only think about it glancingly, in brief bursts, and then quickly jump to something else. It was too weird to be true.

But there were more things in heaven and earth, etc.; and without question there were very intelligent people in his life who believed in this stuff, and acted on those beliefs. That in itself made it real, or something with real effects.

In any case, the trouble would not come to a head while he was out in the Sierras. He would only be gone a week, and Joe had been much the same, week to week, all that winter and spring and through the summer so far.

So Charlie made his preparations for the trip without talking openly to Anna about Joe, and without meeting her eye when she was tired. She too avoided the topic.

It was harder with Joe: "When you going Dad?" he would shout on occasion. "How long? What you gonna do? Hiking? Can I go?" And then when Charlie explained that he couldn't, he would shrug. "Oh well. See you when you get back Dad."

It was heartbreaking.

On the morning of Charlie's departure, Joe patted him on the arm. "Bye Da. Be *careful*," saying it just like Charlie always said it, as a half-exasperated reminder, just as Charlie's father had always said it to him, as if the default plan were to do something reckless, so that one had to be reminded.

Anna clutched him to her. "Be careful. Have fun."

"I will. I love you."

"I love you too. Be careful."

Charlie and Frank flew from Dulles to Ontario together, making a plane change in Dallas.

Frank had had his operation eighteen days before, he said. "So what was it like?" Charlie asked him.

"Oh, you know. They put you out."

"For how long?"

"A few hours I think."

"And after that?"

"Felt fine."

Although, Charlie saw, he seemed to have even less to say than before. So on the second leg of the trip, with Frank sitting beside him looking out the window of the plane, and every page of that day's *Post* read, Charlie fell asleep.

It was too bad about the operation. Charlie was in an agony of apprehension about it, but as Joe lay there on the hospital bed he looked up at his father and tried to reassure him. "It be all right Da." They had attached wires to his skull, connecting him to a bulky machine by the bed, but most of his hair was still unshaved, and under the mesh cap his expression was resolute. He squeezed Charlie's hand, then let go and clenched his fists by his sides, preparing himself, mouth pursed. The doctor on the far side of the bed nodded; time for delivery of the treatment. Joe saw this, and to give himself courage began to sing one of his wordless marching tunes, "Da, da da da, da!" The doctor flicked a switch on the machine and instantaneously Joe sizzled to a small black crisp on the bed.

Charlie jerked upright with a gasp.

"You okay?" Frank said.

Charlie shuddered, fought to dispel the image. He was clutching the seat arms hard.

"Bad dream," he got out. He hauled himself up in his seat and took some deep breaths. "Just a little nightmare. I'm fine."

But the image stuck with him, like the taste of poison. Very obvious symbolism, of course, in the crass way dreams sometimes had—image of a fear he had in him, expressed visually, sure—but so brutal, so ugly! He felt betrayed by his own mind. He could hardly believe himself capable of imagining such a thing. Where did such monsters come from?

He recalled a friend who had once mentioned he was taking St. John's wort in order to combat nightmares. At the time Charlie had thought it a bit silly; the moment you woke up from dreams you knew they were not real, so how bad could a nightmare be?

Now he knew, and finally he felt for his old friend.

So when his old friends and roommates Dave and Vince picked them up at the Ontario airport and they drove north in Dave's van, Charlie and Frank were both a bit subdued. They sat in the middle seats of the van and let Dave and Vince do most of the talking up front. These two were more than willing to fill the hours of the drive with tales of the previous year's work in criminal defense and urology. Occasionally Vince would turn around in the passenger seat and demand some words from Charlie, and Charlie would reply, working to shake off the trauma of the dream and get into the good mood that he knew he should be experiencing. They were off to the mountains— the southern end of the Sierra Nevada was appearing ahead to their left already, the weird desert ranges above Death Valley were off to their right. They were entering Owens Valley, one of the greatest mountain valleys on the planet! It was typically one of the high points of their trips; but this time he wasn't quite into it yet.

In Independence they met the van bringing down the two northern members of their group, Jeff and Troy, and they all wandered the little grocery store there, buying forgotten necessities or delicacies, happy at the sudden reunion of all these companions from their shared youth—a reunion with their own youthful selves, it seemed. Even Charlie felt that, and slowly managed to push the horrible dream away from his conscious awareness and his mood, to forget it. It was, in the end, only a dream.

Frank meanwhile was an easy presence, cruising the tight aisles of the rustic store peering at things, comfortable with all their talk of gear and food and trailhead firewood. Charlie was pleased to see that although he was still very quiet, a tiny little smile was creasing his features as he looked at displays of beef jerky and cigarette lighters and postcards. He looked relaxed. He knew this place.

Out in the parking lot the mountains to east and west hemmed in the evening sky, and told them they were already in the Sierras—or, to be more precise, in the space the Sierras defined, which very much included Owens Valley. To the east the dry White Mountains were dusty orange in the sunset; to the west, the huge escarpment of the Sierra loomed over them like a stupendous serrated wall. Together the two ranges created a sense of the valley as a great roofless room.

The room could have been an exhibit in a museum, illustrating what California had looked like a century before. Around then Los Angeles had stolen the valley's water, as described in the movie *Chinatown* and elsewhere; ironically, this had done the place a tremendous favor, by forestalling subsequent development and making it a sort of time capsule.

They drove the two cars out to the trailhead. The great escarpment fell directly from the crest of the Sierra to the floor of Owens Valley, the whole plunge of ten thousand feet right there before them—one of the biggest escarpments on the face of the planet. It formed a very complex wall, with major undulations, twists and turns, peaks and dips, buttressing ridges, and gigantic outlier masses. Every low point in the crest made for a potential pass into the back country, and many not-so-low points had also been used as cross-country passes. One of the games that Charlie's group of friends had fallen into over the years was that of trying to cross the crest in as many places as they could. This year they were going in over Taboose Pass, "before we get too old for it," as they said to Frank. Taboose was one of what Terry had named the Four Bad Passes (Frank smiled to hear this). They were bad because their trailheads were all on the floor of Owens Valley, and thus about five thousand feet above sea level, while the passes on the crest, usually about ten miles away from the trailheads, were all well over eleven thousand feet high. Thus six thousand vertical feet, usually hiked on the first day, when their packs were heaviest. They had once ascended Baxter Pass, and once come down Shepherd's Pass; only Sawmill and Taboose remained, and this year they were going to do Taboose, said to be the hardest of them all. 5,300 feet to 11,360, in seven miles.

They drove to a little car campground by Taboose Creek and found it empty, which increased their good cheer. The creek itself was almost completely dry, a bad sign, as it drained one of the larger east-side canyons. There was no snow at all to be seen up on the crest of the range, nor over on the White Mountains.

Sacred Space

"They'll have to rename them the Brown Mountains," Troy said. He was full of news of the drought that had been afflicting most of the Sierra for the last few years, a drought that was worse the farther north one went. Troy went into the Sierras a lot, and had seen the damage himself. "You won't believe it," he told Charlie ominously.

They partied through the sunset around a picnic table crowded with gear and beer and munchies. One of the range's characteristic lenticular clouds formed like a spaceship over the crest and turned pale orange and pink as the evening lengthened. Taboose Pass itself was visible above them, a huge U in the crest. Clearly the early native peoples would have had no problem identifying it as a pass over the range, and Troy told them of what he had read about the archeological finds in the area of the pass while Vince barbequed filet mignon and red bell peppers on a thick old iron grate.

Frank prodded the grate curiously. "I guess these things are the same everywhere," he said.

They ate dinner, drank, caught up on the year, reminisced about previous trips. Charlie was pleased to see Vince ask Frank some questions about his work, which Frank answered briefly if politely. He did not want to talk about that, Charlie could see; but he seemed content. When they were done eating he walked up the creekside on his own, looking around as he went.

Charlie then relaxed in the presence of his old friends. Vince regaled them with ever-stranger tales of the L.A. legal system, and they laughed and threw a frisbee around, half-blind in the dusk. Frank came out of the darkness to join them for that. He turned out to be very accurate with a frisbee.

Then as it got late they slipped into their sleeping bags, promising they would make an early start, even, given the severity of the ascent facing them, an actual early start, with alarms set, as opposed to their more usual legendary early start, which did not depend on alarms and could take until eleven or noon.

So they woke, groaning, to alarms before dawn, and packed in a hurry while eating breakfast; then drove up the last gravel road to a tiny trailhead parking lot, hacked into the last possible spot before the escarpment made its abrupt jump off the valley floor. They were going to be hiking up the interior sides of a steep and deep granite ravine, but the trail began by running on top of a lateral moraine which had been left behind by the ravine's Ice Age glacier. The ice had been gone for ten thousand years but the moraine was still perfect, as smooth-walled as if bulldozers had made it.

The trail led them onto the granite buttress flanking the ravine on its right, and they rose quickly, and could see better and better just how steep the escarpment was. Polished granite overhead marked how high the glacier had run in the ravine. The ice had carved a trough in hard orange granite.

After about an hour the trail contoured into the gorge and ran beside the dry creekbed. Now the stupendous orange battlements of the sidewalls of the ravine rose vertically to each side, constricting their view of anything except the sky above and a shrinking wedge of valley floor behind them and below. None of the escarpment canyons they had been in before matched this one for chiseled immensity and steepness.

Troy often talked as he hiked, muttering mostly to himself, so that Charlie behind him only heard every other phrase—something about the great U of Taboose Pass being an ice field rather than just a glacier. Not much of the crest had gotten iced over even at the height of the Ice Age, he said. A substantial ice cap had covered big parts of the range, but mostly to the west of the crest. To the east there had been only these ravine glaciers. The ice had covered what were now the best hiking and camping areas, where all the lakes and ponds had been scooped out of the tops of mostly bare granite plutons. It had been a lighter glaciation than in the Alps, so the tops of the plutons had been left intact for lakes to dot, not etched away by ice until there were only cirques and horns and deep forested valleys. The Alps' heavier snowfall and higher latitude had meant all its high basins had in effect been ground away. Thus (Troy concluded triumphantly) one had the explanation for the infinite superiority of the Sierra Nevada for backpacking purposes.

And so on. Troy was their mountain man, the one whose life was focused on it most fully, and who therefore served as their navigator, gear innovator, historian, geologist, and all-around Sierra guru. He spent a lot of hiking time alone, and although happy to have his friends along, still had a tendency to hold long dialogues with himself, as he must have done when on his solo trips.

Troy's overarching thesis was that if backpacking were your criterion of judgment, the Sierra Nevada of California was an unequaled paradise, and essentially heaven on Earth. All mountain ranges were beautiful, of course, but backpacking as an activity had been invented in the Sierra by John Muir and his friends, so it worked there better than anywhere else. Name any other range and Troy would snap out the reason it would not serve as well as the Sierra; this was a game he and Charlie played from time to time.

"Alps."

"Rain, too steep, no basins, dangerous. Too many people."

"But they're beautiful right?"

"Very beautiful."

"Colorado Rockies."

"Too big, no lakes, too dry, boring."

"Canadian Rockies."

"Grizzly bears, rain, forest, too big. Not enough granite. Pretty though."

"Andes."

"Tea hut system, need guides, no lakes. I'd like to do that though."

"Himalayas."

"Too big, tea hut system. I'd like to go back though."

"Pamirs."

"Terrorists."

"Appalachians."

"Mosquitoes, people, forest, no lakes. Boring."

"Transantarctics."

"Too cold, too expensive. I'd like to see them though."

"Carpathians?"

"Too many vampires!"

And so on. Only the Sierras had all the qualities Troy deemed necessary for hiking, camping, scrambling, and contemplating mountain beauty.

No argument from Charlie. Although he noticed it looked about as dry as the desert ranges to the east. It seemed they were in the rain shadow of the range even here. The Nevada ranges must have been completely baked.

All day they hiked up the great gorge. It twisted and then broadened a little, but otherwise changed little as they rose. Orange rock leaped at the dark blue sky, and the battlements seemed to vibrate in place as Charlie paused to look at them—the effect of his heart pounding in his chest. Trudge trudge trudge. It was a strange feeling, Charlie thought, to know that for the next hour you were going to be doing nothing but walking—and after that hour, you would take a break and then walk some more. Hour following hour, all day long. It was so different from the days at home that it took some getting used to. It took shifting gears. It was in effect a different state of consciousness; only the experience of his previous backpacking trips allowed Charlie to slip back into it so readily. Mountain time; slow down. Pay attention to the rock. Look around. Slide back into the long ruminative rhythms of thought that plodded along at their own pedestrian pace, interrupted often by close examination of the granite, or the details of the trail as it crossed the meager stream which to everyone's relief was making occasional excursions from deep beneath boulderfields; or a brief exchange with one of the other guys, as they came in and out of a switchback, and thus came close enough to each other to talk. In general they all hiked at their own paces, and as time passed, spread out up and down the trail.

A day was a long time. The sun beat down on them from high overhead. Charlie and some of the others, Vince especially, paced themselves by singing songs. Charlie hummed or chanted one of Beethoven's many themes of resolute determination, looping them endlessly. He also found himself unusually susceptible to bad pop and TV songs from his youth; these arose spontaneously within him and then stuck like burrs, for an hour or more, no matter what he tried to replace them with—things like "Red Rubber Ball" (actually a great song) or "Meet the Flintstones"—tromping methodically uphill, muttering over and over "We'll have a gay old—we'll have a gay old—we'll have a gay old time!"

"Charlie please shut up. Now you have me doing that."

"—a three hour tour! A three hour tour!"

So the day passed. Sometimes it would seem to Charlie like a good allegory for life itself. You just keep hiking uphill.

Frank hiked sometimes ahead, sometimes behind. He seemed lost in his thoughts, or the view, and was never particularly aware of the others. Nor did he seem to notice the work of the hike. He drifted up, mouth hanging open as he looked at the ravine's great orange sidewalls.

In the late afternoon they trudged up the final stony rubble of the headwall, and into the pass—or onto it, as it was just as huge as the view from below had suggested: a deep broad U in the crest of the range, two thousand feet lower than the peaks marking each side of the U. These peaks were over a mile apart; and the depression of the pass was also nearly a mile from east to west, which was extremely unusual for a Sierra pass; most dropped away immediately on both sides, sometimes very steeply. Not so here, where a number of little black-rimmed ponds dotted an uneven granite flat.

"It's so big!"

"It looks like the Himalayas," Frank remarked as he walked by.

Troy had dropped his pack and wandered off to the south rise of the pass, checking out the little snow ponds tucked among the rocks. Now he whooped and called them all over to him. They stood up, groaning and complaining, and rubber-legged to him.

He pointed triumphantly at a low ring of stacked granite blocks, set on a flat tuck of decomposed granite next to one of the ponds. "Check it out guys. I ran into the national park archeologist last summer, and he told me about this. It's the foundation of a Native American summer shelter. They built some kind of wicker house on this base. They've dated them as old as five thousand years up here, but the archeologist said he thought they might be twice as old as that."

"How can you tell it's not just some campers from last year?" Vince demanded in his courtroom voice. This was an old game, and Troy immediately snapped back, "Obsidian flakes in the Sierra all come from knapping arrowheads. Rates

71

of hydration can be used to date when the flaking was done. Standard methodology, accepted by all! And—" He reached down and plucked something from the decomposed granite at Vince's feet, held it aloft triumphantly: "Obsidian flake! Proof positive! Case closed!"

"Not until you get this dated," Vince muttered, checking the ground out now like the rest of them. "There could have been an arrowhead-making class up here just last week."

"Ha ha ha. That's how you get criminals back on the streets of L.A., but it won't work here. There's obsidian everywhere you look."

And in fact there was. They were all finding it; exclaiming, shouting, crawling on hands and knees, faces inches from the granite.

"Don't take any of it!" Troy warned them, just as Jeff began to fill a baggie with them. "It screws up their counts. It doesn't matter that there are thousands of pieces here. This is an archeological site on federal land. You are grotesquely breaking the law there, Jeffrey. Citizen's arrest! Vincent, you're a witness to this! What do you mean, you don't see a thing." Then he fell back into contemplating the stone ring.

"Awesome," Charlie said.

"It really gives you a sense of them. The guy said they probably spent all summer up here. They did it for hundreds of years, maybe thousands. The people from the west brought up food and seashells, and the people from the east, salt and obsidian. It really helps you to see they were just like us."

Frank was on his hands and knees to get his face down to

the level of the low rock foundation, his nose inches from the lichen-covered granite, nodding as he listened to Troy. "It's beautiful drywall," he commented. "You can tell by the lichen that it's been here a long time. It's like a Goldsworthy. My Lord. This is a sacred place."

Finally they went back to their packs, put them back on their backs, and staggered down into a high little basin to the west of the pass, where scoops of sand and dwarf trees appeared among some big erratic boulders. The day's hump up the great wall had taken it out of them. When they found a flat area with enough sandy patches to serve as a camp, they sat next to their backpacks and pulled out their warm clothes and their food bags and the rest of their gear, and had just enough energy and daylight left to get water from the nearest pond, then cook and eat their meals. They groaned stiffly as they stood to make their final arrangements, and congratulated each other on the good climb. They were in their bags and on the way to sleep before the sky had gone fully dark.

Before exhaustion knocked him out, Charlie looked over and saw Frank sitting up in his sleeping bag, looking west at the electric blue band of sky over the black peaks to the west. He seemed untired by their ascent, or the sudden rise to altitude; absorbed by the immense spaces around them. Wrapped in thought. Charlie hoped his nose was doing all right. The stars were popping out overhead, swiftly surpassing in number and brilliance any starscapes they ever saw at home. The Milky Way was like a moraine of stars. Sound of distant water clucking through a patch of meadow, the wind in the pines; black spiky horizons all around, the smooth airy gap of the pass behind. It was a blessing to feel so tired in such a place. They had made the effort it took to regather, and here they were again, in a place so sublime no one could truly remember what it was like when they were away, so that every return had a sense of surprise, as if re-entering a miracle. Every time it felt this way: it was the California that could never be taken away.

Except it could.

Charlie had, of course, read about the ongoing drought that had afflicted the Sierra for the last few years, and he was also familiar with the climate models which suggested that the Sierra would be one of those places most affected by the global rise in temperature. California's wet months had been November through April, with the rest of the year as dry as any desert. A classic Mediterranean climate. Even during the Hyperniño this pattern had tended to endure, although in El Niño conditions more rain fell in the southern half of the state and less in the northern half, with the Sierras therefore getting a bit of both. In the past, however, whatever the amount of precipitation, it had fallen on the Sierra in the form of snow; this had created a thick winter snowpack, which then took most of the summer to melt. That meant that the reservoirs in the foothills got fed a stream of melting snow at a rate that could then be dispersed out to the cities and farms. In effect the Sierra snowpack itself had been the ultimate reservoir, far bigger than what the artificial ones behind dams in the foothills could hold.

Now, however, with global temperatures higher, more of

the winter precipitation came down as rain, and thus ran off immediately. The annual reservoir of snow was smaller, even in good years; and in droughts it hardly formed at all.

California was in an uproar about this. New dams were being built, including the Auburn dam, located right on an earthquake fault; and the movement to remove the Hetch Hetchy dam had been defeated, despite the fact that the next reservoir down the Tuolomne had the capacity to hold all Hetch Hetchy's water. State officials were also begging Oregon and Washington to allow a pipeline to be built to convey water south from the Columbia River. The Columbia dumped a huge amount into the Pacific, one hundred times that of the maximum flow of the Colorado River, and all of it *unused*. It was immoral, some said. But naturally the citizens of Oregon and Washington had refused to agree to the pipeline, happy at a chance to stick it to California. Only the possibility that many Californians would then move north, bringing their obese equities with them, was causing any of them to reconsider their stance. But of course clear cost-benefit analysis was not the national strong suit in any case, so on the battle would go for the foreseeable future.

In any case, no matter what political and hydrological adjustments were made in the lowlands, the high Sierra meadows were dying.

This was a shock to witness. It had changed in the three years since Charlie had last been up. He hiked down the trail on their second morning with a sinking feeling in his stomach, able to cinch the waistbelt of his pack tighter and tighter.

They were walking down the side of a big glacial gorge to the

John Muir Trail. When they reached it, they headed north on it for a short distance, going gently uphill as the trail followed the south fork of the Kings River up toward Upper Basin and Mather Pass. As they hiked it became obvious that the high basin meadows were much too dry for early August. They were desiccated; ponds were often pans of cracked dirt. Grass was brown. Plants were dead: trees, bushes, ground cover, grasses. Even mosses. There were no marmots to be seen, and few birds. Only the lichen seemed okay—although as Vince pointed out, it was hard to tell. "If lichen dies does it lose its color?" No one knew.

After a few of these discouraging miles they turned left and followed an entirely dry tributary uphill to the northwest, aiming at the Vennacher Needle, a prominent peak, extremely broad for a needle, as Vince pointed out. "One of those famous blunt-tipped needles. One of those spherical needles."

Up and up, over broken granite, much whiter than the orange stuff east of Taboose Pass. This was the Cartridge Pluton, Troy told them as they ascended. A very pure bubble of granite. The batholith, meaning the whole mass of the range, was composed of about twenty or thirty plutons, which were the individual bubbles of granite making up the larger mass. The Cartridge was one of the most clearly differentiated plutons, separated as it was by glacial gorges from all the plutons around it. There was no easy way to get over its curving outer ridge into Lakes Basin, the high granite area atop the mass. They were hiking up to one of these entry points now, a pass called Vennacher Col.

The eastern approach to the col got steeper as they

approached it, until they were grabbing the boulders facing them to help pull themselves up. And the other side was said to be steeper! But the destination was said to be fine: a remote basin, empty of trails and people, and dotted with lakes—many lakes—and lakes so big, Charlie saw with relief as he pulled into the airy pass, that they had survived the drought and were still there. They glittered in the white granite below like patches of cobalt silk.

Far, far below: for the western side of Vennacher Col was a very steep glacial headwall—in short, a cliff. The first five hundred vertical feet of their drop lay right under their toes, an airy nothing.

Troy had warned them about this. The Sierra guidebooks all rated this side of the pass class 3. In scrambling or (gulp) climbing terms, it was the crux of their week. Normally they avoided anything harder than class 2, and now they were remembering why.

"Troy?" Vince said. "Why are we here?"

"We are here to suffer," Troy intoned.

"Bayer Aspirin, it was your idea to do this, what the fuck?"

"I came up this way with these guys once. It's not as bad as it looks."

"You think you came up it," Charlie reminded him. "It was twenty years ago and you don't remember exactly what you did."

"It had to be here."

"Is this class 2?" Vince demanded.

"This side has a little class 3 section that you see here."

"You're calling this cliff little?"

"It's mostly a class 2 cliff."

"But don't you rate terrain by the highest level of difficulty?"

"Yes."

"So this is a class 3 pass."

"Technically, yes."

"Technically? You mean in some other sense, this cliff is not a cliff?"

"That's right."

The distinction between class 2 and class 3, Charlie maintained, lay precisely in what they were witnessing now: on class 2, one used one's hands for balance, but the terrain was not very steep, so that if one fell one could not do more than crack an ankle, at most. So the scrambling was fun. Whereas class 3 indicated terrain steep enough that although one could still scramble up and down it fairly easily, a fall on it would be dangerous—perhaps fatally dangerous—making the scramble nerve-racking, even in places a little terrifying. The classic description in the Roper guidebook said of it, "like ascending a steep narrow old staircase on the outside of a tower, without banisters." But it could be much worse than that. So the distinction between class 2 and class 3 was fuzzy in regard to rock, but very precise emotionally, marking as it did the border between fun and fear.

In this case, the actual class 3 route down the cliff, as described by the guidebooks and vaguely remembered by Troy from twenty years before, was a steep incision running transversely down the face from north to south. A kind of gully; and they could see that if they could get into this gully, they would be protected. The worst that could happen then was that they might slide down the gully a ways if they slipped.

But getting into the gully from the top was the trick. The class 3 moment, in effect. And no one liked the look of it, not even Troy.

The five old friends wandered back and forth anxiously on the giant rocks of the pass, peering down at the problem and talking it over. Frank sat off to the side, looking around at the view. The top of the inner wall of the slot was a sheer cliff and out of the question. The class 3 route appeared to require downclimbing a stack of huge boulders topping the outer wall of the slot.

No one was happy at the prospect of getting down the outer wall's boulder stack. With backpacks or without, it was very exposed. Charlie wanted to be happy with it, but he wasn't. Troy had come up it once, or so he said, but going up was generally easier than going down. Maybe Troy could now downclimb it; and presumably Frank could, being a climber and all. But the rest of them, no.

Charlie looked around to see what Frank might say. Finally he spotted him, sitting on the flat top of one of the pass rocks, looking out to the west. It seemed clear he didn't care one way or the other what they did. As a climber he existed in a different universe, in which class 3 was the stuff you ran down on after climbing the real thing. Real climbing *started* with class 5, and even then it only got what climbers would call serious at 5.8 or 5.9, or 5.10 or 5.11. Looking at the boulder stack again, Charlie wondered what 5.11 would look like—or feel like to be on it! Never had he felt less inclined to take up rock climbing than he did at that moment.

But Frank didn't look like he was thinking about the descent at all. He sat on his block looking down at Lakes Basin, biting off pieces of an energy bar. Charlie was impressed by his tact, if that's what it was. Because they were in a bit of a quandary, and Charlie was pretty sure that Frank could have led them into the slot, or down some other route, if he had wanted to. But it wasn't his trip; he was a guest; and so he kept his counsel.

Or maybe he was just spacing out, even to the point of being unaware there was any problem facing the rest of them. He sat staring at the view, chewing ruminatively, body relaxed. A man at peace. Charlie wandered up the narrow spine of the pass to his side.

"Nice, eh?"

"Oh my, yes," Frank said. "Just gorgeous. What a beautiful basin."

"It really is."

"It's strange to think how few people will ever see this," Frank said. He had not volunteered even so much as this since they had met at Dulles, and Charlie crouched by his side to listen. "Maybe only a few hundred people in the history of the world have ever seen it. And if you don't see it, you can't really imagine it. So it's almost like it doesn't exist for most people. So really this basin is a kind of secret. A hidden valley that you have to search for. And even then you might never find it."

"I guess so," Charlie said. "We're lucky."

"Yes."

"How's your head feel up here?"

"Oh good. Good, sure. Interesting!"

"No post-op bleeding, or psychosis or anything?"

"No. Not as far as I can tell."

Charlie laughed. "That's as good as."

He stood and walked down the spine to where the others were continuing to discuss options.

"What about straight down from the lowest point here?" Vince demanded.

Charlie objected, "That won't work—look at the drop." He still wanted to want to try the boulder stack.

"But around that buttress down there, maybe," Dave pointed out. "Something's sure to go around it."

"Why do you say that?"

"I don't know. Because it always does in the Sierra."

"Except when it doesn't!"

"I'm going to try it," Jeff declared, and took off before anyone had time to point out that since he was by far the most reckless among them, his ability to descend a route said very little about it as far as the rest of them were concerned.

"Don't forget your comb!" Vince said, in reference to a time when Jeff had used a plastic comb to hack steps up a vertical snowbank no one else had cared to try.

Ten minutes later, however, he was a good portion of the way down the cliff, considerably off to the left as they looked down, where the steepness of the rock angled outward, and looked quite comfy compared to where they were.

He yelled back up at them, "Piece of cake! Piece of cake!"

"Yeah right!" they all yelled.

But there he was, and he had done it so fast that they had to try it. They found some very narrow ledges hidden under the buttress, trending down and left, and by holding onto the broken white granite of the wall next to their heads, and making their way carefully along the ledges and down from ledge to ledge, they had all soon followed Jeff to the less steep bulge in the cliff, and from there each took a different route to a horrible jumble of rocks in a flat trough at the bottom.

"Wow!" Charlie said as they regathered on a big white rock among the rest, next to a little bowl of caked black dust that had once been a pool of water. "That was class 2! I was wrong. It wasn't so bad! Wasn't that class 2?" he asked of Troy and Frank.

"It probably was," Troy said.

"So you guys just discovered a class 2 route on a wall that all the guidebooks call class 3!"

"How could that happen?" Vince wondered. "Why would we be the ones to find it?"

"We were desperate," Troy said, looking back up. From below the cliff looked even steeper than it had from above.

"That's probably actually it," Charlie said. "The class ratings up here have mostly been made by climbers, and when they came up to this pass they probably saw the big slot in the face, and ran right up it without a second thought, because it's so obvious. The fact it was class 3 meant nothing to them, they didn't care one way or the other, so they rated it 3, which is right if you're only talking about the slot. They never even noticed there was a much trickier class 2 line off to the side, because they didn't need it."

Frank nodded. "Could be."

"We'll have to write to the authors of the guidebooks and see if we can get them to relist Vennacher Col as class 2! We can call the route the Jeffrey Dirretissimma."

"Very cool. You do that."

"Actually," Vince pointed out, "it was my refusal to go down the slot that caused Jeff to take the new route, and I'm the one that spotted it first, so I'm thinking it should be called the Salami Dirretissima. That has a better ring to it anyway."

That night, in a wonderful campsite next to the biggest of the Lake Basin's lakes (none had names), their dinner party was extra cheery. They had crossed a hard pass—an impossible pass—and were now in the lap of beauty, lying around on ground pads dressed like pashas in colorful silken clothing, drinking an extra dram or two of their carefully hoarded liquor supplies, watching the sun burnish the landscape. The water copper, the granite bronze, the sky cobalt. On the northern wall of the basin a single tongue of cloud lapped up the slope like some sinuous creature, slowly turning pink. Each of them cooked his own dinner, on various kinds of tiny backpacking stoves, and in various styles of backpacking fare: Dave and Jeff sticking with the old ramen and mac-and-cheese, Vince with the weirdest freeze-dried meals currently available at REI; Troy downing a glop of his own devising, a mixture of powders from the bins of his food co-op, intensely healthy and fortified; Charlie employing the lark's-tongues-in-aspic theory of extreme tastiness, in a somewhat vain attempt to overcome the appetite suppression that often struck him at altitude. Frank appeared to favor a diet that most resembled Troy's, with bars and bags of nuts and grains supplying his meals.

After dinner the Maxfield Parrish blues of the twilight gave way to the stars, and then the Milky Way. The moon would not rise for a few hours, and in the starlight they could still see the strange tongue of low cloud, now gray, licking the north wall of the basin. The lake beside them stilled to a starry black mirror. Quickly the cold began to press on the little envelopes of warmth their clothes created, and they slid into their sleeping bags and continued to watch the tiny stove pellet fire that Dave kept going, feeding it from time to time with the tiniest of twigs and pine needles.

The conversation wandered, and sometimes grew ribald: Dave was outlining an all-too-convincing biological basis for the so-called midlife crisis, and general confessions of inappropriate lust for young women were soon augmented by one or two individual case studies of close calls, at work or in the gym. Oh my God. Laughter in the dark, and some long silences too.

Voices by starlight. But it's stupid. It's just your genes making one last desperate scream when they can feel they're falling apart. Programmed cell death. Apoptosis, you bet. They want you to have more kids to up their chance of being immortal, they don't give a shit about you or your actual happiness or anything.

If you're just fooling around, if you don't mean to leave your wife and go with that person, then it's like masturbating in someone else's body.

Yuck! Jesus, yuck!

Hoots of horrified hilarity, echoing off the cliffs across the lake. That's so gross I'll never again be able to think about having an affair!

So I cured you. So now you're old. Your genes have given up.

My genes will never give up.

The little stove pellet burned out. The hikers went quiet and were soon asleep, under the great slow wheel of the stars.

The next day they explored the Lakes Basin, looking into a tributary of it called the Dumbbell Basin, and dropping to the Y-shaped Triple Falls on Cartridge Creek, before turning back up toward the head of the basin proper. It was a beautiful day, the heart of the trip, just as it was the heart of the pluton, and that pluton the heart of the Sierra itself. No trails, no people, no views out of the range. They walked on the heart of the world.

On such days some kind of freedom descended on them. Mornings were cold and clear, spent lazing around their sleeping bags and breakfast coffee. They chatted casually, discussed the quality of their night's sleep. They asked Charlie about what it was like to work for the president: Charlie gave them his little testimonial. "He's a good guy," he told them. "He's not a normal guy, but he's a good one. He's still real. He has the gift of a happy temperament. He sees the funny side of things." Frank listened to this closely, head cocked to one side.

Once they got packed up and started, they wandered apart, or in duos, catching up on the year's news, on the wives and kids, the work and play, the world at large. Stopping frequently to marvel at the landscapes that constantly shifted in perspective around them. It was very dry, a lot of the fellfields and meadows were brown, but the lakes were still there and their borders were green as of old. The distant ridges; the towering thunderheads in the afternoons; the height of the sky itself; the thin cold air; the pace of the seconds, tocking at the back of the throat; all combined to create a sense of spaciousness unlike any they ever felt anywhere else. It was another world.

But this world kept intruding.

Their plan was to exit the basin by way of Cartridge Pass, which was south of Vennacher Col, on the same border ridge of the pluton. This pass had been the original route for the Muir Trail; the trail over it had been abandoned in 1934, after the CCC built the replacement trail over Mather Pass. Now the old trail was no longer on the maps, and Troy said the guidebooks described it as being gone. But he didn't believe it, and in yet another of his archeological quests, he wanted to see if they could relocate any signs of it. "I think what happened was that when the USGS did the ground check for their maps in 1968, they tried to find the trail over on the other side, and it's all forest and brush over there, so they couldn't pick it up, and they wrote it off. But over on this side there's nothing but rock up near the top. I don't believe much could happen to a trail up there. Anyway I want to look."

Vince said, "So this is another cross-country pass, that's what you're saying."

"Maybe."

So once again they were on the hunt. They hiked slowly uphill, separating again into their own spaces. " 'Now I know you're not the only starfish in the sea!' Starfish? How many other great American songs are about starfish, I ask you? 'Yeah, the worst is over now, the morning sun is rising like a *red, rubber ball!*' "

Then on the southeast slope of the headwall, where the maps showed the old trail had gone, their shouts rang out once more. Right where one would have hiked if one were simply following the path of least resistance up the slope, a trail appeared. As they hiked up, it became more and more evident, until high on the headwall it began to switchback up a broad talus gully that ran up between solid granite buttresses. In that gully the trail became as obvious as a Roman road, because its bed was made of decomposed granite that had been washed into a surface and then in effect cemented there by years of rain, without any summer boots ever breaking it up. It looked like the nearly concretized paths that landscapers created with decomposed granite in the world below, but here the raw material had been left in situ and shaped by feet. People had only hiked it for some thirty or forty years—unless the Native Americans had used this pass too—and it was another obvious one, and near Taboose, so maybe they had—in which case people had hiked it for five or ten thousand years. In any case, a great trail, with the archeological component adding to the sheer physical grandeur of it.

"There are lost trails like this on an island in Maine," Frank remarked to no one in particular. He was looking around with what Charlie now thought of as his habitual hiking expression. It seemed he walked in a rapture.

The pass itself gave them long views in all directions—north back into the basin, south over the giant gap of the Muro Blanco, a granite-walled canyon. Peaks beyond in all directions.

After a leisurely lunch in the sun, they put on their packs and started down into the Muro Blanco. The lost trail held, thinning through high meadows, growing fainter as they descended, but always still there.

But here the grass was brown. This was a south-facing slope, and it almost looked like late autumn. Not quite, for autumn in the Sierra was marked by fall colors in the ground cover, including a neon scarlet that came out on slopes backlit by the sun. Now that same ground cover was simply brown. It was dead. Except for fringes of green around drying ponds, or algal mats on the exposed pond bottoms, every plant on this south-facing slope had died. It was as burnt as any range in Nevada. One of the loveliest landscapes on the planet, dead before their eyes.

They hiked at their different paces, each alone on the rocky rumpled landscape. Bench to bench, terrace to terrace, graben to graben, fellfield to fellfield, each in his own private world.

Charlie fell behind the rest, stumbling from time to time in his distress, careless of his feet as his gaze wandered from one little eco-disaster to the next. He loved these high meadows with all his heart, and the fellfields between them too. Each had been so perfect, like works of art, as if hundreds of meticulous bonsai gardeners had spent centuries clipping and arranging each watercourse and pad of moss. Every blade of grass deployed to best effect, every rock in its proper place. It had never occurred to Charlie that any of it could ever go away. And yet here it was, dead.

Desolation filled him. It pressed inside him, slowing him down, buffeting him from inside, making him stumble. Not the Sierra. Everything living that he loved in this Alpine world would go away, and then it would not be the Sierra. Suddenly he thought of Joe and a giant stab of fear pierced him like a sword, he sank back and sat on the nearest rock, felled by the feeling. Never doubt our emotions rule us; and no matter what we do, or say, or resolve, a single feeling can knock us down like a sword to the heart. A dead meadow—image of a black crisp on a bed—Charlie groaned and put his face to his knees.

He tried to pull himself back into the world. Behind him Frank was still wandering, lonely as a cloud, deep in his own space; but soon he would catch up.

Charlie took a deep breath, pulled himself together. Several more deep breaths. No one would ever know how shaken he had been by his thoughts. So much of life is a private experience.

Frank stood over him. He looked down at him with his head cocked. "You okay?"

"I'm okay. You?"

"I'm okay." He gestured around them. "Quite the drought."

"That's for sure!" Charlie shook his head violently from side to side. "It makes me sad—it makes me afraid! I mean—it looks so bad. It looks like it could be gone for good!"

"You think so?"

"Sure! Don't you?"

Frank shrugged. "There's been droughts up here before. They've found dead trees a couple hundred feet down in Lake Tahoe. Stuff like that. Signs of big droughts. It seems like it dries out up here from time to time."

"Yes. But—you know. What if it lasts a hundred years? What if it lasts a thousand years?"

"Well, sure. That would be bad. But we're doing so much to the weather. And it's pretty chaotic anyway. Hopefully it will be all right."

Charlie shrugged. This was thin comfort.

Again Frank regarded him. "Aside from that, you're okay?"

"Yeah sure." It was so unlike Frank to ask, especially on this trip. Charlie felt an urge to continue: "I'm worried about Joe. Nothing in particular, you know. Just worried. It's hard to imagine, sometimes, how he is going to get on in this world."

"Your Joe? He'll get on fine. You don't have to worry about him."

Frank stood over Charlie, hands folded on the tops of his walking poles, looking out at the sweep of the Muro Blanco, the great granite canyon walled by long cliffs of white granite. At ease; distracted. Or so it seemed. As he wandered away he said over his shoulder, "Your kids will be fine."

HERMIE

by Nathaniel Rich

Vermin, heights, thunderstorms, airplanes, wide-open spaces, commitment—they don't get to me, not at all, but public speaking is another thing altogether. The Introduction to Marine Biology lecture I give to my freshmen every year is enough to rattle me, so you can imagine how I felt in the moments before my speech at the Eighteenth International Conference of Limnology and Oceanology in Salzburg this year. Fortunately I have developed a practice that has served me well in these moments. Fifteen minutes before I have to go on, I make a trip to the restroom, where I wash my hands and recite several passages from the paper I'm to deliver. Then I close my eyes and repeat to myself, like a mantra, three words: Calm Blue Ocean. Calm Blue Ocean. Calm Blue Ocean. When I open my eyes—well, I may still have the flutters but I'm as ready as I'm ever going to be.

So as Arnie Lundtfelt was coming to the end of his discussion of organochlorine contamination of the Bering Sea's Steller sea lion pup population, I quietly exited the conference room and made my way to the head. I've always found the restrooms at Sheraton Hotels to be consistently clean, well-attended, and capacious; I have observed this to be true in Lyon, San Diego, Toronto, and even Hanoi, at the Third Annual Polycheate Conference, a few years back. The Salzburg bathroom was no exception: the mirror was unsmudged, there were no puddles around the urinals, and the bank of three sinks was a pure white porcelain. I say this only to emphasize how quickly, and with what a sense of shock, I noticed, perched next to the rim of the middle sink, a giant Coenobita clypeatus. That is to say, a hermit crab.

I didn't recognize him at first. Perhaps it was because he had changed his shell. Gone was the buyscon spiratum I remembered so well: a perfect pear whelk, with alternating bands of burnt orange and nacre, polished by the tide to a delicate glow; its long tapering stem; its tight spiral apex; and the open fold revealing a darker orange interior—an elegant, if compact, home. In its place was a filthy, unwieldy, carbuncled husk, to which there clung small bits of wet garbage and sea gunk. On closer examination it was clear that two common shells— one dark brown, the other a dreary shade of green—had been roughly fused together. There is no scientific term for such a monstrosity.

From the shell's opening there emerged two cautious antennae, testing the air. Then several furry claws, bronzed by age, tapped the white counter with their hardened pincers. With a sudden display of agility, the animal pivoted, scraping his shell against the porcelain. His black beady eyes fixed directly on mine. I gasped.

"Hello, old friend." The voice was hoarse, scratchy. I glanced around the bathroom—I even ducked down and looked for feet in the stalls—but I knew it was pointless. I was the only person there.

"Ah. So you don't recognize me."

I stared at the hermit crab. His claws were drawn up beneath his shell, folded like the legs of a kneeling child.

"I'm sorry," I said. I kept looking around, but to be honest I was just trying to buy myself some time. The voice was coming from within the shell.

"I don't blame you," said the hermit crab. One of his antennas gestured behind him toward the mirror. "I can't even recognize myself."

"I just—I'm sorry—"

"It's Hermie."

I couldn't believe it.

"I know, I don't look the same. Or sound the same. But a lot of years have passed since our summers in Sarasota. You don't look the same either, by the way."

This was true. The last time I had seen him I was roughly four feet tall. My voice hadn't yet broken, and I had yet to lose my baby fat. Now I had a full beard.

"Do you remember?" said Hermie. "The dunes of Siesta Key, on Turtle Beach?"

I grinned, despite myself. "How could I forget? It's just that—well, it's been a long time."

"So you remember our days on the shore?"

"Sure I do. In fact, I now study coastal regions for a living. That's the reason I'm here, in Salzburg—"

"What about The King's Castle?"

I smiled at the memory.

"The King's Castle," I said. "I forgot we called it that. It took the whole afternoon to construct, because I only had that little red pail with the broken handle, but by the end we had battlements, an arcaded pavilion, even a gatehouse."

"Yes, and remember the high tower where you put my throne, and the waterslide that you pushed me down, into the moat, and . . ." He trailed off as that long-ago day in the sun seemed to wash over him.

"It's good to see you, Hermie."

There was an awkward silence.

"What about Man-Buried-Alive?" I said.

"Ha!" said the crab. "That was a good one. I was always a little bit scared at first, but then I would dig my way out."

"Except that one time."

"Well that was not fair, putting the pail over the sand. I assumed it was night, and that you had left me behind."

"Oh, I didn't keep you under too long. As soon as I heard your claws scratching against the plastic, I let you out."

"I think you might have waited a few minutes. I could hear you cackling. But then you set me free, and I loved you all the same."

"That was one of our best adventures." I smiled at the memory.

94

"There were also the seaweed salads that you made for me," said Hermie, laughing. "With sea salt dressing."

"You had quite an appetite."

Hermie squealed. "It was delicious!"

"No wonder you had to find yourself a new shell!"

Hermie's laughter stopped.

"That's not the reason I have a new shell."

"No," I said. "Of course it's not."

"Turtle Beach—it's completely gone."

"I'm sorry to hear that."

"They tore it up. Exploded the beach and inserted columns. They put up an apartment building much too close to the water. This was some time after you left."

"I see."

"Then the hurricanes came. They got worse and worse. They swallowed up the beaches whole." His voice got very quiet. "Why did you stop coming to Turtle Beach, anyway? Where did you go?"

"I don't know," I said, but of course I did. I just couldn't bear to tell him the truth. I did not stop coming to Turtle Beach, at least not at first. I just stopped visiting Hermie. My mother explained to me that ten-year-old boys were too old to play with talking hermit crabs, or any other imaginary friends. A few years later I went off to boarding school, and then to college. I never returned to Sarasota.

"Can't you pick up and move to another beach?" I asked.

"I tried—first to Venice, then Casey Key, then Manasota. The whole key is disappearing. Everywhere there is sticky water, sharp unnatural pebbles, and invisible seaweed that tastes awful."

"I'm actually working on this very issue. The sustainability of coastal environments. Erosion. Rising sea levels. The title of my talk today, in fact, is 'Differential seed and seedling predation by coenobita: impacts on coastal composition.'"

Hermie didn't seem to know how to respond. "I have no place to go, old friend."

I started to wonder how Hermie could have gotten into the bathroom in the first place. The windows were sealed; he was too large to enter through the sink drains, or the urinal. And how did he get from Sarasota to Salzburg?

"What about the rest of the old gang?" I asked. "Stella the Starfish? Ernie the Urchin? Gulliver?"

"They're dead. Long dead. Every last one of them. Clammy and all her daughters too. I found Clammy myself. Her shell— it's too horrible to say." His voice cracked. "Her shell had turned green. She had been poisoned."

"Oh. I'm very sorry to hear that."

Hermie propped himself up with his claws, a gesture that appeared to require heavy physical exertion. A gesture of supplication.

"Do you remember how we would bob in the ocean?" he said. "How you would hold me in the palm of your hand, and when a wave went over your head, you would lift me above the surface, in the air?"

I nodded, but I didn't know how to respond. With a quick motion—I couldn't help myself—I checked the time on my cell phone. There were only five minutes left before my speech.

"I'm sorry to say this, but I have to go give my talk presently."

"I wondered," said Hermie, his ancient voice animated by an irrational optimism, "have you found us a new place?"

"Excuse me? I don't know what you mean."

"A new home? A safe, clean home, where we could play in the sea forever more?"

"I—I don't know what to say. I live in Philadelphia now. With my wife and young daughter."

"A daughter? How old is she?"

"She's three," I said. I didn't like this line of conversation.

"Does she love hermit crabs, and other sea creatures?"

"She's never been to the ocean."

Hermie's antennas lowered to the counter, slowly, with incalculable sadness.

"Maybe I can live with you?" His voice was small, frail.

"I don't know. It's just that—well, my wife is allergic to shellfish."

"My! I hope you wouldn't consider serving me to her. After all we've been through together . . ."

"No, of course not, I didn't mean to imply—"

"Just think of all the fun adventures we'd have. Your daughter could join us, if you like. Really. I wouldn't mind. We could go again in search of the Dum Dum Tree. Remember the Dum Dum Tree?"

"First of all, there's no way that airport security would let you through."

He stared at me, his eyes fixed like little black stones. But I realized he couldn't possibly be crying. There are no tear ducts on a hermit crab's eyestalk.

"I'm sorry, Hermie."

He didn't speak for some time. His knuckles scraped against the white counter, as if he were trying to dig a hole in the porcelain. I glanced again at my phone. Two minutes left.

"I have to go."

"Old friend?" Hermie's voice was resigned, stiff. Feeble. "Before you leave, can you just do me a single favor?"

My stomach dropped.

"What is it?"

"Can you carry me into the toilet? It took a long time for me to crawl over here. It was difficult to climb up the sink. I don't know how I might possibly get back down again. I could fall. My shell is fragile."

Of course! The toilet—that was how he had gotten here. The explanation relieved me. I suppose, in the initial surprise of seeing Hermie again, I had momentarily lost my ability to think logically.

Delicately I picked up Hermie. His shell was beaded with moisture, and gave off a faint, metallic scent, like flaked rust. He withdrew his claws so as not to scrape the skin of my palm. He was surprisingly light, as if his shell was filled with nothing more than air. I opened the door of the nearest stall and bent down next to the toilet.

"On the seat here is fine," he said. "Thank you."

I rested him there.

"One last thing," he said. "When I sink to the bottom, would you be so kind as to flush?"

I nodded. "Bye, Hermie."

Shakily he raised one of his claws in valediction. Then he pivoted himself and, with a shove, pushed himself over the rim. The water splashed up. Hermie sunk to the bottom of the bowl. I looked at him one last time, then I flushed. The force of the jets lifted him. In that moment there was something about the colors of his shell, as he spun around the bowl, that brought back with sudden clarity the King's Castle and Man Buried Alive, Ernie and Clammy, the Dum Dum Tree and the Kaleidoscope Fountain. I was back on Turtle Beach, holding my red plastic pail, my feet breaded with the fine yellow sand, the rush of the tide powerful in my ears, the sun hot on my face.

Then it was gone. I lowered the lid. It seemed like the right thing to do.

If I can say so myself, I think the paper was a success. I might just submit it to the *Hydrobiology Review*. I didn't even feel nervous when I delivered it. There were nearly twenty-five people in attendance and later, at the cocktail hour, no less than four of them offered me their compliments.

DIARY OF AN INTERESTING YEAR

by Helen Simpson

12th February 2040
My thirtieth birthday. G gave me this little spiral-backed note-book and a biro. It's a good present, hardly any rust on the spiral and no water damage to the paper. I'm going to start a diary. I'll keep my handwriting tiny to make the paper go further.

15th February 2040
G is really getting me down. He's in his element. They should carve it on his tombstone—"I Was Right."

23rd February 2040
Glad we don't live in London. The Hatchwells have got cousins staying with them, they trekked up from Tottenham (three days). Went round this afternoon and they were saying the thing that finally drove them out was the sewage system— when the drains packed up it overflowed everywhere. They

said the smell was unbelievable, the pavements were swimming in it, and of course the hospitals are down so there's nothing to be done about the cholera. Didn't get too close to them in case they were carrying it. They lost their two sons like that last year.

"You see," G said to me on the way home, "capitalism cared more about its children as accessories and demonstrations of earning power than for their future."

"Oh shut up," I said.

2nd March 2040
Can't sleep. I'm writing this instead of staring at the ceiling. There's a mosquito in the room, I can hear it whining close to my ear. Very humid, air like filthy soup, plus we're supposed to wear our facemasks in bed too but I was running with sweat so I ripped mine off just now. Got up and looked at myself in the mirror on the landing—ribs like a fence, hair in greasy rats' tails. Yesterday the rats in the kitchen were busy gnawing away at the breadbin, they didn't even look up when I came in.

6th March 2040
Another quarrel with G. OK, yes, he was right, but why crow about it? That's what you get when you marry your tutor from Uni—wall-to-wall pontificating from an older man. "I saw it coming, any fool could see it coming especially after the Big Melt," he brags. "Thresholds crossed, cascade effect, hopelessly optimistic to assume we had till 2060, blahdy blahdy blah, the

plutonomy as lemming, democracy's massive own goal." No wonder we haven't got any friends.

He cheered when rationing came in. He's the one that volunteered first as car-share warden for our road; one piddling little Peugeot for the entire road. He gets a real kick out of the camaraderie round the standpipe.

—I'll swop my big tin of chickpeas for your little tin of sardines.

—No, no, my sardines are protein.

—Chickpeas are protein too, plus they fill you up more. Anyway, I thought you still had some tuna.

—No, I swopped that with Violet Huggins for a tin of tomato soup.

Really sick of bartering, but hard to know how to earn money since the internet went down. "Also, money's no use unless you've got shedloads of it," as I said to him in bed last night. "The top layer hanging on inside their plastic bubbles of filtered air while the rest of us shuffle round with goitres and tumours and bits of old sheet tied over our mouths. Plus, we're soaking wet the whole time. We've given up on umbrellas, we just go round permanently drenched." I only stopped ranting when I heard a snore and clocked he was asleep.

8th April 2040
Boring morning washing out rags. No wood for hot water, so had to use ashes and lye again. Hands very sore even though I put plastic bags over them. Did the facemasks first, then the rags from my period. Took forever. At least I haven't got to do

nappies like Lexi or Esme, that would send me right over the edge.

27th April 2040

Just back from Maia's. Seven months. She's very frightened. I don't blame her. She tried to make me promise I'd take care of the baby if anything happens to her. I havered (mostly at the thought of coming between her and that throwback Martin— she'd got a new black eye, I didn't ask). I suppose there's no harm in promising if it makes her feel better. After all it wouldn't exactly be taking on a responsibility—I give a new baby three months max in these conditions. Diarrhoea, basically.

14th May 2040

Can't sleep. Bites itching, trying not to scratch. Heavy thumps and squeaks just above, in the ceiling. Think of something nice. Soap and hot water. Fresh air. Condoms! Sick of being permanently on knife edge re pregnancy.

Start again. Wandering round a supermarket—warm, gorgeously lit—corridors of open fridges full of tiger prawns and fillet steak. Gliding off down the fast lane in a sports car, stopping to fill up with thirty litres of petrol. Online, booking tickets for *The Mousetrap*, click, ordering a crate of wine, click, a holiday home, click, a pair of patent leather boots, click, a gap year, click. I go to iTunes and download *The Marriage of Figaro*, then I chat face to face in real time with G's parents in Sydney. No, don't think about what happened to them. Horrible. Go to sleep.

21st May 2040

Another row with G. He blew my second candle out, he said one was enough. It wasn't though, I couldn't see to read any more. He drives me mad, it's like living with a policeman. It always was, even before the Collapse. "The Earth has enough for everyone's need, but not for everyone's greed," was his favourite. Nobody likes being labelled greedy. I called him Killjoy and he didn't like that. "Every one of us takes about 25 thousand breaths a day," he told me. "Each breath removes oxygen from the atmosphere and replaces it with carbon dioxide." Well, pardon me for breathing! What was I supposed to do—turn into a tree?

6th June 2040

Went round to the Lumleys for the news last night. Whole road there squashed into front room, straining to listen to radio—batteries very low (no new ones in the last govt delivery). Big news though—compulsory billeting next week. The Shorthouses were up in arms, Kai shouting and red in the face, Lexi in tears. "You work all your life" etc., etc. What planet is he on. None of us too keen, but nothing to be done about it. When we got back, G checked our stash of tins under the bedroom floorboards. A big rat shot out and I screamed my head off. G held me till I stopped crying then we had sex. Woke in the night and prayed not to be pregnant, though God knows who I was praying to.

12th June 2040

Visited Maia this afternoon. She was in bed, her legs have swollen up like balloons. On at me again to promise about the baby

105

and this time I said yes. She said Violet Huggins was going to help her when it started—Violet was a nurse once, apparently, not really the hands-on sort but better than nothing. Nobody else in the road will have a clue what to do now we can't google it. "All I remember from old films is that you're supposed to boil a kettle," I said. We started to laugh, we got a bit hysterical. Knuckledragger Martin put his head round the door and growled at us to shut it.

1st July 2040
First billet arrived today by army truck. We've got a Spanish group of eight including one old lady, her daughter and twin toddler grandsons (all pretty feral), plus four unsmiling men of fighting age. A bit much since we only have two bedrooms. G and I tried to show them round but they ignored us, the grandmother bagged our bedroom straight off. We're under the kitchen table tonight. I might try to sleep on top of it because of the rats. We couldn't think of anything to say—the only Spanish we could remember was *muchas gracias*, and as G said, we're certainly not saying *that*.

2nd July 2040
Fell off the table in my sleep. Bashed my elbow. Covered in bruises.

3rd July 2040
G depressed. The four Spaniards are bigger than him, and he's worried that the biggest one, Miguel, has his eye on me (with reason, I have to say).

4th July 2040
G depressed. The grandmother found our tins under the floor-boards and all but danced a flamenco. Miguel punched G when he tried to reclaim a tin of sardines and since then his nose won't stop bleeding.

6th July 2040
Last night under the table G came up with a plan. He thinks we should head north. Now this lot are in the flat and a new group from Tehran promised next week, we might as well cut and run. Scotland's heaving, everyone else has already had the same idea, so he thinks we should get on one of the ferries to Stavanger then aim for Russia.

"I don't know," I said. "Where would we stay?"

"I've got the pop-up tent packed in a rucksack behind the shed," he said. "Plus our sleeping bags and my wind-up radio."

"Camping in the mud," I said.

"Look on the bright side," he said. "We have a huge mort-gage and we're just going to walk away from it."

"Oh shut up," I said.

17th July 2040
Maia died yesterday. It was horrible. The baby got stuck two weeks ago, it died inside her. Violet Huggins was useless, she didn't have a clue. Martin started waving his Swiss penknife around on the second day and yelling about a Caesarean, he had to be dragged off her. He's round at ours now drinking the

last of our precious brandy with the Spaniards. That's it. We've got to go. Now, says G. Yes.

1st August 2040

Somewhere in Shropshire, or possibly Cheshire. We're staying off the beaten track. Heavy rain. This notebook's pages have gone all wavy. At least biro doesn't run. I'm lying inside the tent now, G is out foraging. We got away in the middle of the night. G slung our two rucksacks across the bike. We took turns to wheel it, then on the fourth morning we woke up and looked outside the tent flap and it was gone even though we'd covered it with leaves the night before.

"Could be worse," said G. "We could have had our throats cut while we slept."

"Oh shut up," I said.

3rd August 2040

Rivers and streams all toxic—fertilisers, typhoid, etc. So, we're following G's DIY system. Dip billycan into stream or river. Add three drops of bleach. Boil up on camping stove with t-shirt stretched over billycan. Only moisture squeezed from the t-shirt is safe to drink; nothing else. "You're joking," I said, when G first showed me how to do this. But no.

9th August 2040

Radio news in muddy sleeping bags—skeleton govt obviously struggling, they keep playing *The Enigma Variations*. Last night they announced the end of fuel for civilian use and the compulsory disabling of all remaining civilian cars. As from now we must all stay at home, they said, and not travel without permission. There's talk of martial law. We're going cross-country as much as possible—less chance of being arrested or mugged—trying to cover ten miles a day but the weather slows us down. Torrential rain, often horizontal in gusting winds.

16th August 2040
Rare dry afternoon. Black lace clouds over yellow sky. Brown grass, frowsty grey mould, fungal frills. Dead trees come crashing down without warning—one nearly got us today, it made us jump. G was hoping we'd find stuff growing in the fields, but all the farmland round here is surrounded by razor wire and armed guards. He says he knows how to grow vegetables from his allotment days, but so what. They take too long. We're hungry *now*, we can't wait till March for some old carrots to get ripe.

22nd August 2040
G broke a front crown cracking a beechnut, there's a black hole and he whistles when he talks. "Damsons, blackberries, young green nettles for soup," he said at the start of all this, smacking his lips. He's not so keen now. No damsons or blackberries, of course—only chickweed and ivy.

He's just caught a lame squirrel so I suppose I'll have to do something with it. No creatures left except squirrels, rats and pigeons, unless you count the insects. The news says they're full of protein, you're meant to grind them into a paste, but so far we haven't been able to face that.

24th August 2040

We met a pig this morning. It was a bit thin for a pig, and it didn't look well. G said, "Quick! We've got to kill it."

"Why?" I said. "How?"

"With a knife," he said. "Bacon. Sausages."

I pointed out that even if we managed to stab it to death with our old kitchen knife, which looked unlikely, we wouldn't be able just to open it up and find bacon and sausages inside.

"Milk, then!" said G wildly. "It's a mammal, isn't it?"

Meanwhile the pig walked off.

25th August 2040

Ravenous. We've both got streaming colds. Jumping with fleas, itching like crazy. Weeping sores on hands and faces—the news says, unfortunate side effects from cloud-seeding. What with all this and his toothache (back molar, swollen jaw) and the malaria, G is in a bad way.

27th August 2040

Found a dead hedgehog. Tried to peel off its spines and barbecue it over the last briquette. Disgusting. Both sick as dogs. Why did I used to moan about the barter system? Foraging is MUCH MUCH worse.

29th August 2040

Dreamed of Maia and the penknife and woke up crying. G held me in his shaky arms and talked about Russia, how it's the new land of milk and honey since the Big Melt. "Some really good farming opportunities opening up in Siberia," he said through chattering teeth. "We're like in *The Three Sisters*," I said. " 'If only we could get to Moscow'. Do you remember that production at the National? We walked by the river afterwards, we stood and listened to Big Ben chime midnight." Hugged each other and carried on like this until sleep came.

31st August 2040

G woke up crying. I held him and hushed him and asked what was the matter. "I wish I had a gun," he said.

15th September 2040

Can't believe this notebook was still at the bottom of the rucksack. And the biro. Murderer wasn't interested in them. He's turned everything else inside out (including me). G didn't have a gun. This one has a gun.

19th September 2040

M speaks another language. Norwegian? Dutch? Croatian? We can't talk, so he hits me instead. He smells like an abandoned fridge, his breath stinks of rot. What he does to me is horrible. I don't want to think about it, I won't think about it. There's a tent and cooking stuff on the ground, but half the time we're up a tree with the gun. There's a big plank platform and a tarpaulin roped to the branches above. At night he pulls the rope ladder up after us. It's quite high, you can see for miles. He uses it for storing stuff he brings back from his mugging expeditions. I'm surrounded by tins of baked beans.

3rd October 2040
M can't seem to get through the day without at least two blow-jobs. I'm always sick afterwards (sometimes during).

8th October 2040
M beat me up yesterday. I'd tried to escape. I shan't do that again, he's too fast.

14th October 2040
If we run out of beans I think he might kill me for food. There were warnings about it on the news a while back. This one wouldn't think twice. I'm just meat on legs to him. He bit me all over last night, hard. I'm covered in bite marks. I was literally licking my wounds afterwards when I remembered how nice the taste of blood is, how I miss it. Strength. Calf's liver for iron. How I haven't had a period for ages. When that thought popped out I missed a beat. Then my blood ran cold.

15th October 2040
Wasn't it juniper berries they used to use? As in gin? Even if it was I wouldn't know what they looked like, I only remember mint and basil. I can't be pregnant. I won't be pregnant.

112

Diary of an Interesting Year

17th October 2040
Very sick after drinking rank juice off random stewed herbs. Nothing else, though, worse luck.

20th October 2040
Can't sleep. Dreamed of G, I was moving against him, it started to go up a little way so I thought he wasn't really dead. Dreadful waking to find M there instead.

23rd October 2040
Can't sleep. Very bruised and scratched after today. They used to throw themselves downstairs to get rid of it. The trouble is, the gravel pit just wasn't deep enough, plus the bramble bushes kept breaking my fall. There was some sort of body down there too, seething with white vermin. Maybe it was a goat or a pig or something, but I don't think it was. I keep thinking it might have been G.

31 October 2040
This baby will be the death of me. Would. Let's make that a subjunctive. "Would," not "will."

7th November 2040
It's all over. I'm still here. Too tired to

8th November 2040
Slept for hours. Stronger. I've got all the food and drink, and the gun. There's still some shouting from down there but it's weaker now. I think he's almost finished.

9th November 2040
Slept for hours. Fever gone. Baked beans for breakfast. More groans started up just now. Never mind. I can wait.

10th November 2040
It's over. I got stuck into his bottle of vodka, it was the demon drink that saved me. He was out mugging—left me up the tree as usual—I drank just enough to raise my courage. Nothing else worked so I thought I'd get him to beat me up. When he came back and saw me waving the bottle he was beside himself. I pretended to be drunker than I was and I lay down on the wooden platform with my arms round my head while he got the boot in. It worked. Not right away, but that night.

Meanwhile M decided he fancied a drink himself, and very soon he'd polished off the rest of it—over three-quarters of a bottle. He was singing and sobbing and carrying on, out of his tree with alcohol, and then, when he was standing pissing off the side of the platform, I crept along and gave him a gigantic shove and he really was out of his tree. Crash.

13th November 2040
I've wrapped your remains in my good blue shirt; sorry I couldn't let you stay on board, but there's no future now for any baby above ground. I'm the end of the line!

This is the last page of my thirtieth birthday present. When I've finished it I'll wrap the notebook up in six plastic bags, sealing each one with duct tape against the rain, then I'll bury it in a hole on top of the blue shirt. I don't know why as I'm not mad enough to think anybody will ever read it. After that I'm going to buckle on this rucksack of provisions and head north with my gun. Wish me luck. Last line: good luck, good luck, good luck, good luck, good luck.

NEWROMANCER

by Toby Litt

18.8.2040

"Oi, you!"

He means me.

"Yes, I mean you, young feller-me-laddie."

Should have stuck to the backstreets, but I thought the peasouper was thick enough to keep me hidden.

"Right. See this building here?"

How could I miss it?

"This building is officially on fire."

I look up at the vast concrete frontage of 300 Oxford Street, the former John Lewis building. 300 Oxford Street is definitely *not* on fire, although I know exactly what the Fire Warden means.

And thank the Lord it *is* a Fire Warden, not a Crip. Our boys in blue have some major firepower, and dogs. Major dogs.

"What on Earth do you think you're up to, breaking the curfew? Don't you know there's a war on?"

This Fire Warden is albino, pug-ugly, and sounds like he's enjoying 2040 much more than any of the rest of his (I'd guess) forty years.

He has an automatic shoved down the waistband of his trousers. From what I can see of the handle, this looks real enough, but most of the Wardens' weapons are fake—carved out of wood then painted gray. The man's helmet is definitely papier mâché and chickenwire—I can see the crosshatching on the underbrim. Can't see much else, though, because he's shining his torch right in my eyes. It's been a long time since I faced a light so bright. This must be what proper squint-making sunshine was like.

"Now, look lively and sharpish and all that malarkey and get yourself back down the underground while this raid's still on."

But now, silly me, I'm gazing straight up—the sky is a dead gray, and completely silent. No planes. No air-raid. The only sounds I can hear are horses' hooves, thudding on the manure that covers the Tarmac.

"Are you being disrespectful of me, sonny jim? Because if you are, I'll have your guts for starters."

At least he's not searching me. If he saw what I had on under this greatcoat, I'd be in the cells prontissimo. (Utility wear? Me?) He hasn't even noticed the boots.

I know I must speak, say something credible to give me a cover story, tell him I'm out getting meds for my old dad, and so I open my mouth and run.

"Stop!" shouts the Fire Warden. "Stop, or I'll shoot!"

Visibility is down to about twenty feet. I have at least another ten to go before I'm out of his sight, and another hundred before I'm out of earshot. I pray I was right about his gun. We'll soon find out.

"I'm drawing my weapon! This is your last chance!"

I speed up—sprinting into the gray.

"Bang!" he shouts, and I send thanks to God. It's a fake! "You have officially been shot. Come back. Bang! Bang! You have now officially been shot three times!"

I keep running as the albino's voice gets higher and higher. I am not playing their silly little wargame, and it really annoys him. The last thing he shouts is "If you come back now, you will receive free medical care!"

For just a moment I almost think about turning back. What if he's telling the truth? I could get these lesions on my legs fixed up. They could check out my eyes, which I'm sure need specs from all this peering through the gloom. Maybe someone could tell me exactly what this black stuff I've been coughing up means.

But I'm a sensible boy, and I run away from the agents of the law as fast as I bloody well can. I listen for sounds behind me, and what I hear is a whistle which, a couple of seconds later, is answered by one whistle, then another. I slow from a sprint to a run, plunging deeper into the lovely gray fog.

Think I'm safe now. Can walk again, catch my puff. Don't want to seem out of sorts when I make my big entrance at The Blitz. That's *my* Blitz, *our* Blitz, no way *their* Blitz, which started ten days ago, and is just so so faux. I mean, whoever thought of forcing the entire country to reenact the events of 1940 *exactly* a hundred years to the day later? What Whitehall wonker came up with that? Chap seriously needs his head removing. I mean, yes, it's ten percent more carbon-efficient than going ahead with 2040, as previously planned. And, yes, it gives the authorities a good excuse to enforce the blackout that was bound to happen anyway. Yes, it means that "Dig for Victory" and "Make-Do and Mend" posters can be plastered over those empty billboards. But also, yes, it means that no one anything like young is allowed to be anything like young.

No drugs. No dancing. No decent clothes. No loud music. These things are Earthkillers so these things must be banned.

Not that the oldschool Blitz (September 1940–May 1941) was like this. I've been doing my research, and from what I can make out, London was a pretty swinging town back then, give or take the odd sprinkling of TNT. If you weren't bombed out by Hitler, you were bombed out on benzedrine. Dark alleys were full of courting couples—home leave squaddies and randy Land Girls up for the night.

What we're being forced to go through today by this bunch of Tescommunists is the cleaned-up revisionist version. And it's not as if the Walmarxists would do anything different, so don't go thinking your vote could change stuff.

But our Blitz is keeping it real. Instead of 1940, we've defaulted to 1980. And we fully intend drugs, dancing, and most of all decent clothes. The loud music, I'm afraid, has been sacrificed to practicality. But we have a way round that. You'll see.

I hope you'll see.

Because clippety-clop and cloppety-clip along with scritch and then scratch and what could that be? Snarl, from somewhere behind me. And a good old-fashioned woof!—oh crap. Not great. Snarl snarl! Those would be major dogs. Clippety-clop! Those would be horses.

And these would be Crips.

"Okay," I scream, backed up against a shopfront. "Call them off."

They're a pitbull-alsatian cross. There are three of them. They are absolutely ruining my trousers.

"That's him! That's the one."

"Hello, again," I say.

The Fire Warden is sat up behind the Crip sergeant, on a huge grey horse. Another couple of horse-riding boys in blue are behind them.

The Crip sergeant whistles, and the dogs leave off my legs.

"Man say you been shot."

"I suppose so," I say.

"You best go hospital," he says. "Get fix up."

"I shall do," I say.

"Police hospital," he says.

I am in the back of one of their wagons, being guarded by a female Crip. Her gun is real. For five minutes she hasn't stopped staring at my trousers, which might be rescuable with a little of my own make-do and mend.

"Where were you going?" the Crip asks. "Dressed up like that?"

My costume has been revealed. I'm wearing—brace yourself—a double-breasted grandpa-collar white cotton shirt with scarlet trim and silver buttons, sixteen-pleat black trousers with scarlet piping tucked into burgundy pixie boots, about seven strings of pearls, my great-grandmother's best onyx brooch, and in my bag I have a Tyrolean hat with a blue feather on the side. Now, when was the last time you saw an outfit like that?

"Where were you going?" she asks again.

Again I don't reply.

"Go on," she says. "You can tell me. I'll keep quiet."

I shoot her a look—yeah, like I'd trust you. But the look I sneak at the same time has a kicker. She's really very cute. And quite stylish, too. I can see that her hair, beneath her helmet, is cut pretty sharp. Is that homemade gel I detect? Surely she's breaking some regulations here.

"Was it The Blitz?" she asks.

"How do you know that?" I blurt, freaked out. "No-one's meant to know that." No one but us kids, I mean.

"Would you take me?" she asks.

What?

"I really want to go," she says. "I have the clothes. I've just never met anyone who would take me. And I get off shift in, like, half an hour."

"I've been shot," I say. "I'm not going anywhere. I'm probably bleeding to death. Officially."

She glances up through the grille, toward where the driver is sitting. So far, he's whipped the horses about every ten steps. We're not going slowly.

"I can get you out," she says.

I don't seem to have many other options. But I know I'm taking a big risk. The Crips would love to shut down on The Blitz. Every time we meet, we use up precious natural resources—that's according to them. I mean, even the word "pop" suggests waste.

"Tell him to pull over," I say.

She rattles her gun-barrel on the bars. "Hold up!" she shouts.

"Tell him to open the door."

Two minutes later, I am alone with her in the fog.

"Thank you," I say.

"My pleasure," she replies. "I'm Sharice."

"Ferdinand," I say, giving my club-name.

"First, I need to get changed," says Sharice. "Can't go there dressed like this, can I?"

"How do I know this isn't some set-up?" I ask.

"I got you out, didn't I?" Sharice says.

My face says, Convince me.

"Okay, then," she says. "I'll let you go. You can just walk off now. Bye-bye."

"Bye-bye," I say, and walk off.

But ten feet into the fog I change my mind, turn round and walk back. I like Sharice. And I especially like the way she's smiling at me now, as if she's five and I'm Santa Claus.

Let's see what her clothes are like. If they're obviously some lame attempt to go undercover, I'll dump her as soon as we get back on the street.

Sharice's flat is halfway up Centerpoint. But I can't check the view because all the windows are covered in blackout material. And there won't be a view anyway, because of the fog.

"Make yourself comfortable," she says.

So I sit on her sofa and drink a mug of water and stare at the dead television while she goes into the bedroom, closes the door and gets dressed by the light of her torch.

Half an hour I wait. But it's worth it. When Sharice comes out, she's a full-on harlequin. Big diamonds of cloth from neck to ankle—red, blue, black and yellow. She shines the torch up and down herself. I particularly like up.

"How long did it take you to make that?"

"A month," she says. "Since I first heard 'Ashes to Ashes'."

Our anthem—well, that and "Fade to Gray."

"And you heard it where?" There's no TV since the phoney war started, and the BBC is playing no music but classical and swing.

"Someone in the cells was singing it. He was wearing a bandana, eyeshadow, the lot. I asked him what it was. He told me."

I like Sharice.

"Do you have make-up?" I ask. She shows me the contents of her little bag.

Newromancer

I love Sharice.

"Follow me," I say.

The club should be at 4 Great Queen Street, but if we held it there the Crips would find it easily. Instead, it's somewhere nearby which changes every time. Tonight, it's in a basement off Parker Street.

The doorman's name is Jim and he calls himself Steve but everyone knows him as Jack. As we sashay up, Jack's doing his party-piece. He hands a small mirror to some poor bedraggled wannabe wearing a polkadot ra-ra skirt and asks, "Would *you* let you in?" Some people will never get it.

Jack knows me, admires Sharice when she opens her coat, and we're waved through.

As we walk down the narrow staircase, bad paintings on the wall, Sharice squeezes my arm. I think I have a date for the evening.

"Wow," she says.

Wow is pretty much the effect we were aiming for.

The dance floor is completely full. There's no DJ—we can't risk loud music. The Heavy Metal Kids up in Covent Garden get closed down almost as soon as they start up. Five minutes' headbanging tops, then the Crips are on them. Same with the Grungers, down by the river. Mosh, cosh, bish-bash-bosh— game over. We're subtle, though.

Some people sing lead vocal. Some do backing. Some do the synths. Some do the synth-drums. Between us, we have a repertoire of about fifty songs. All the classix nouveaux. (Though nothing by Classix Nouveaux.)

The moment we enter, the sound of this particular crowd is "To Cut a Long Story Short."

Sharice gives a whoop that is very uncool, very unCrip, and makes me think, Dalek, I love you.

We head for the toilets and do our make-up, side by side. I am quivering. There's nothing quite like an eyelid brushed with fear. Sharice helps me get the blusher right. (Screw Planet Earth.) I put on my hat, she adjusts it. Then she takes me by the hand and leads me to the dance floor. Fah fah fah fah fashion!

Everyone looks, and I mean *everyone*.

Five minutes, then it's over. But they are the best five minutes of my life (so far).

Jack runs in and shouts, "Crips!"

"They followed us!" I say. "You set this up."

I look at Sharice, expecting to see her smirking. She looks terrified.

"No!" she says. "I'd've known."

You can't act that kind of fear.

Three major dogs scrabble down the stairs. Legs follow them, legs attached to Crips.

Say hello, wave goodbye.

"Come on," I shout, grabbing Sharice by the hand.

We always have a getaway. This time, it's through a ventilation duct in the kitchen. Someone spent two days screwing a ladder into the aluminium. And that someone was me.

Jack leads the way. I let Sharice go after him. The footholds hold. A major dog sprints into the kitchen. I'm up off the ground, but it still gets its teeth into my trousers. Again.

I try to climb, but the dog's really heavy, and it's not letting go.

Then I hear a bang, a real one, and the dog falls down in its own red splatter.

"Come on," shouts Sharice, sticking the gun back into its hiding place.

"Thanks," I say.

We make it out onto the street, harlequin and me, and we peg it back to her flat.

I don't know why, but we laugh all the way.

"What about the bullet?" I ask, when we finally get our puff back. We're on her sofa. "Forensics and whatnot. They'll come for you."

"That wasn't my weapon," Sharice says. "Officially."

She gets it out and shows it to me.

"Got it on a raid the other week," she says.

I'm almost as impressed as I was by the make-up.

"How did they find the club?" I ask.

"Don't know," she says. "But it wasn't us."

"How can you be sure?"

"They'd be here already," she replies with a smile.

This seems logical.

"What shall we do now?" I ask.

"Looks like it's another quiet night in," she says.

We sit and stare at the television, screen the color of a dead sky.

THE SIPHONERS

by David Mitchell

Of all the folktales collected by the authors in the Autonomous Kurdish Region during 1998–99, the following modification of the Thoms-Bredon Cluster 14b (*On the Inadvisability of Geronticide*) [Narr. Ukbar Kishkiev /male /c.75 yrs /farmer /Guurjev Valley /1999 /trans. Avril Bredon and Bruno Thoms from Kurdish] illustrates best how an archetypal wisdom-narrative (one found in cultures as diametric as West Greenland Inuit [La Pointe & Cheng 1928], the Solomon Islands [Daphne Ng 1966] and Central African Republic [Coupland-Weir 1989]) can be mutated by the host-culture's folkways, topography and belief-hierarchies:

Here's a story I had from my wrinkled old aunt, who used to tell it as she worked on her loom, *click-clacketty, click-clacketty, click-clacketty*. Once upon a time there was a land called the Country of Youth where it was the law to give every man and woman a bottle of sleeping poison on the morning they turned sixty years of age. "The Elderly," said the law, "have used up their allotted time. Why should we feed those wrinkled parasites while young, vigorous workers go hungry? Nature Herself culls the old: and we should, too." And so, from the lowliest ragman to the Emperor himself, dwellers of the Country of Youth put their affairs into order ahead of time, and drank the poison before the sun set on their sixtieth birthday. The village or ward headman would then write the words "Honourably at Rest" on the family register. But woe betide any violators of the law! Offenders were hanged alongside their eldest child, and the whole family was dubbed "Parasites" and chased away. Little wonder that the Sixty Years Law was very, very seldom broken.

Now, outside a poor village between a bleak marsh and a blue forest in the Country of Youth, there lived a handsome young woodcutter called Haji. Haji's parents had both died of marsh-fever when he was a babe-in-arms, so the orphaned boy had been raised by his wise grandmother. As the old woman's fifty-ninth, and final, summer passed, Haji grew troubled. *Grandmother*, the young man reasoned, *spent her life caring for me, and teaching me everything I know. How can it be right that she is now tossed aside like a worn-out broom?* Haji built a cabin in the secret deeps of the blue forest. Shortly before harvest, when his grandmother was due to receive her sleeping potion, Haji revealed his plan. "Grandmother, there's a cabin for you in a safe place, in the woods. Please, go into hiding there." At first the old woman refused, frightened of the danger to her grandson if the plot was discovered. But Haji was a determined young man. "The Sixty Year Law is a law of man, Grandmother: what about the law of God, written in our hearts?" Finally, the old woman was won over, and three days later, grim-faced Haji went to the headman's house with his grandmother's blood-soaked old robe. "I found this," said Haji, "in the clearing where grandmother was checking our partridge traps. Wolves, I fear." The headman was a lazy drunken sot who never dreamt the blood was from a suckling pig. Where, after all, could a white-haired old woman hide in the Country of Youth?

Well, summer passed, and autumn rusted the valleys. Raids by bandits over the mountain border had ruined the harvest in that region, so the Emperor decided that before winter closed the passes, he would raise a mounted army

A clattering pan on a stone floor tells me that Bruno is up. I bookmark my spot in our magnum opus, stow my precious reading glasses on the shelf, grab my stick and hobble down the hallway before he has the chance to hurt himself. By the exercise bicycle—used as a coat-stand for most of our marriage— Bruno's trousers lay discarded. I smell, and then see, that he didn't use the privy. Another chore for the morning ahead: at least he didn't step in the mess like yesterday. In the kitchen Bruno is inspecting the fridge's innards, as if it were not a dead cupboard for turnips donated by Finbar but that cabinet of refrigerated wonders we all used to take for granted. "I was searching *every*where for you, Paola." He calls me Paola on good days: on less lucid ones, he just gazes through me.

It's early, so I still have energy to say that I'm Avril, that Paola was his first wife, that Paola passed away many years ago.

"Why's"—my half-naked husband blinks—"the Internet down?"

"We've had no Internet for eight years, Bruno."

For whose sake, I wonder, do I try to tether him to reality?

"How can I do research without Internet access?"

"Put this on—" I take off my dressing gown "—it's chilly."

He allows me to feed his limp arms into the sleeves.

I remember dressing Calvin when he was little . . .

. . . a balloon of grief inflates in my throat, and hurts.

Poor, poor Avril . . . shall we have a little cry?

Bruno frowns. "I'm expecting an email from Fran Worcester!"

Here we go again, for—literally?—the thousandth time.

"She's told the Vice-Chancellor to cut our funding, the witch!"

"Bruno, it's 2033: Fran Worcester's dead; the Vice-Chancellor's dead; our Uni was burnt by Rapturists—" I draw breath and wonder, as ever, where to stop? *Economics has eaten itself; dementia is eating you; climate change has crippled global agriculture; our government only has the means to hold the Cordon because Jīndàn-TransUral needs order on their farm.*

Then I hear men outside, and horse's hoofs.

Must be Finbar. I grab my sheepskin cardigan.

*　　*　　*

132

On the ruckled yard that was once a patio, I find a cart made out of an old boat and car wheels, two Shire horses eating from a nose-bag, and one-two-three-four-five-six-seven strangers—all male. Where to begin? Two intruders are siphoning the paraffin from our tank into large plastic tubs; one perches on the Mitsubishi—now a henhouse—writing something; another minds the horses; and the last three stand guard with guns cocked my way. Army hand-me-downs are in evidence, but the gang's piercings and insouciance all say "Casual Militia." It's hard to guess ages in these feral times: the horse-minder might be as young as twelve or thirteen. They are unfazed by an elderly householder wielding a walking stick, and my sternest voice wavers, rather: "What's going on here, exactly?"

"We ownin' vis jooce Ol'lady," states a jowly one in pungent dialect.

"You can bloody well *un*own it, and pour it back again!"

"Nohcandu Ol'lady. DisGov's requissyin' illegal stockpiles."

"This 'stockpile' is our *legal* quota. Less than five hundred liters."

"More'n elsewheres now'days 'tis." This gunman is pocked with smallpox. "S'tember's tanker's a No-Show at Terminal. Norf o'Cordon, I seen folk get spiked for a ten-liter placky o'jooce."

Spurt by spurt, my paraffin is vanishing: I resort to bluff. "Listen: Captain Oscar Boru of the District Government happens to be my son-in-law, and if you know what's good for you . . ."

Their swapped smiles take the steam out of my sentence.

The one on the Mitsubishi speaks. "Mrs Bredon, am I right?"

I'm surprised by his cultured tone. " 'Professor' Bredon."

"Your neighbor," he nods toward Finbar's, "gave us your name. He reckoned the lads would be less trigger-jumpy once we knew you're no threat." He's about thirty—the age Calvin would be—and his demeanor (and Chinese Burberry flak-jacket) mark him out as leader. "Regarding Oscar Boru, Professor: you must be the fiftieth nearest and dearest of the good captain we've spoken to this week. The joke is that Boru's our main customer—even the DG platoons are zip out of fuel. Hinterland's hogging every last drop." He slaps the plastic tanks. "This'll shore up law and order."

"You're gangsters," I fix his eye, "without official sanction."

"Official," he tilts his head left and right, "unofficial: come *on.*"

"Thieves and thugs," I grip my stick, "plain and simple."

"Fink *we're* fugs?" The jowly lieutenant's smile is what Bruno used to call "Post-Dental Age." "Juss ya wait fo'va Jackdaws."

He's trying to scare me. We live south of the Cordon.

The trees clack and grunt. A horse urinates.

"This fuel's ours," states the leader. "Go back indoors."

"Would *you* take orders from trespassing bandits?"

"Look," he says, "nobody wants to hurt you, but our job—"

"*You* look, Che Guevara: winter's round the corner; my husband and I are in our sixties and we *need* that fuel; so if you think of yourself as a human being, listen to your conscience and put it *back.*"

"Y'oughta gra'itood," says a siphoner, "w'aint takin' y'eats."

"Sixty years' a crack o'whip," says another. "I'll dead by sixty, I'll."

Their lack of compassion is stony and without cracks.

I address the leader. "You're committing an immoral act."

"Here's morality: oil's at three thousand dollars a barrel, in those dwindling zones where prices still mean anything. And we've got dependents, too. Our children will be manning the Cordon, ten years from now. This fuel improves our chances of having a future, of sorts."

"That's just—" what's the right word? "—sophistry." Oh, what's the use? It's over their heads. "You won't get off the Peninsula. We look after our own out here."

"Oha fink we *will* get off okay." Jowls cocks his semi-auto.

"Whassa Sophie's Tree, Wyatt?" asks the boy with the horses.

" 'Sophistry'," says the platoon leader. "Waster lingo. It means 'slick bullshit.' Greek etymology, right, Professor?' He mocks my condescension. "My mum was a—" he opens sarcastic quote marks "—a 'lexicographer'."

Sycamore leaves scurry around our ankles, rat-like.

"So you have a mother, too?" I change tack. "Tell me, if—"

There's a panicky yell of "Va top winder! Sniper!"

Swing and a swivel and a blur and weapons clicking—

I turn around: Bruno is struggling to open the back window.

"Don't shoot!" I'm an old woman shouting in an awful dream where air is noise and my voice is feeble. "We don't have any—"

Crack-bang! A crater appears two meters from Bruno's head, the dirty-laundry sky fills with crows and croaks, the horses shy and the chickens go mental. Incredibly—or not—Bruno hasn't noticed his danger, and carries on fiddling with the window-catch, slack-jawed. I notice that I'm shrieking at a lanky militia-man whose crucifix swings loose: "He hasn't got a *weapon* he's *harmless* don't fire don't *fire!*"

The Crucifix guy looks around at the leader, Wyatt.

Wyatt's watching Bruno, along his handgun's line of fire.

"My husband has Alzheimer's," I plead. "We don't keep guns."

My heartbeat's throbbing so hard my chest cavity feels bruised.

After a sick moment the leader, Wyatt, nods: "Stand down."

Now I snarl at the Crucifix gunman: "You almost *killed* him!"

"Fat chance." The smallpox-scarred one sniggers. "Jeez'd miss a cow at ten paces."

"T'was *forty* paces t'was! An'ya *know* t'was Oshi Whynot."

Bruno, meanwhile, has wrestled open the window. "Paola! Where were you? Are these drop-outs from IT, here to fix the Internet?"

Feeling shame is stupid, and unfair on Bruno, yet I do.

"We are, Sir," Wyatt calls up. "Won't take a jiffy—some joker installed a Californian RBR sequencer, to cut corners. We only use Indian-mades: see you another five years, even on max-hot-tasking."

Bruno nods once. "Ah. Good. Not before time."

He shuts the window and retreats into the blank dark.

Feeling gratitude is stupid, too: especially as the siphoning tube goes limp. That's it. Our fuel's gone. What now? Back to firewood, peat: back to the Middle Ages, step by step.

I'm empty. "How do you people sleep at night?"

Wyatt approaches me. "Professor, I have a gift and some news."

"Yeah? I'll take five hundred liters of paraffin, please."

"First, the gift." From a pocket he removes a tiny clear plastic box.

My fingers recognize the box first. "Two spearmint Tic-Tacs?"

"Mercy beans." The soldier says it like it's nothing special.

"Take your 'gift' back. I don't need suicide pills. We've—"

"Chuck them if you want, but you should hear the news."

"We've survived this long: we'll survive—"

"The Cordon's shifting, Professor: eighty clicks south."

His soft voice cushions the impact of the meaning: at first.

Something plastic falls at my feet: Wyatt stoops for the box.

"The District," I'm saying, "won't abandon the Peninsula!"

Wyatt straightens up and sighs. "Some planner at Jīndàn-TransUral in Petersburg or Beijing surveyed their six.thousand acres on a sat-map; reckoned, *Well, that's not worth the ammo or the manpower*; and it's a done deal. Our Government gets told, not consulted about it."

"So we're just being thrown to the wolves?"

"Yer'd stand more chance," Jeez the Crucifix sniffs, "if *t'was* wolves an'not Jackdaws, Ol'lady."

The steep heath, the sloughing sea, the horizon's a ghostly line.

"So . . . at our ages," I'm saying, "my husband and I are refugees?"

Wyatt holds my eye. "The New Cordon will have an immigration bar."

"This country has been our home for a quarter-century."

"It's not to do with citizenship or ethnicity: it's your age."

I unwrap this riddle and find something terrible. "No: no. They can't keep out the *elderly*?"

Wyatt looks away and looks back. Calvin used to do that, before breaking bad news. "Thirty-five years old for men, Professor, and thirty for women. They have shiny new Chinese chromo-testers at the checkpoints: one dab of saliva and they know your age to within seven days."

"And . . . so . . . well . . . what are *we* supposed to do?"

Ever so gently, Wyatt puts the Tic-Tac box into my hand.

Bruno's snoring, snottily. He's catching a cold. I file his toenails, discolored like rhino horn, and the daylight dies. I usually go to sleep with the sun—once the solar-lamp dies, there's no spare—but tonight I take it to my study. The Siphoners left a grim prognosis after they'd vanished down the track. Finbar and Ann—in their late fifties, also unwanted by the New Cordon—dropped by afterwards. We hatched plots to keep our spirits up. Finbar has one final tranche of fuel for his boat, stored in an old copper mine-shaft: but get real, where would we go? Drift up to the Faroes, like a Rapturist in his faux-medieval coracle, trusting in the breath of Providence? What about Bruno? What would *I* be if I just abandoned him? Wyatt was right: the one place the Jackdaws won't find us, and that's inside a mercy bean. What will I do? Sip nettle tea, retrieve my reading glasses and retreat into volume three of Avril Bredon's and Bruno Thoms' best-known contribution to the now-extinct discipline of anthropology.

Where was I?

Well, summer passed, and autumn rusted the valleys. Raids by bandits over the mountain border had ruined the harvest in that region, so the Emperor decided that before winter closed the passes, he would raise a mounted army to root out this scourge. Every village in the Country of Youth was to send ten men, and now that Haji's household consisted of one, he was the first to be chosen. When Haji's grandmother, safe and warm in her distant cabin, learnt the news, she told Haji this: "The Emperor's a fool. Those mountains could swallow up twenty armies, and when the snows come, it's worse. Here's how you survive. Ride the dun mare to war, but take her colt along, too. At the river on the border, kill the colt. Do this, and with God's grace you'll come home alive."

A horseman in the Emperor's army, Haji heeded his grandmother's advice. At the border crossing, he slit the colt's throat, ignoring the mare's grief and his fellow-soldiers' bafflement. The army rode into the hostile mountains, but the bandits melted away. After three days' riding, the Emperor's forces were ambushed in a tangled valley. Many of Haji's companions were slain in the storm of crossbolts, but the survivors fought back with discipline, cunning and ferocity, and the Emperor's men finally won that bloodiest of days. That night, however, winter pounced: a screaming blizzard confined the army to their tents and makeshift shelters for a week. The wounded perished, an unlucky few were driven mad, the weaker horses froze to death, and food ran out. On the seventh day the skies cleared, but that unmapped world was smothered in snow. Wolves, crows and probably new groups of bandits were gathering, and nobody knew the road home. Haji now remembered his grandmother's advice and begged the Emperor's aide-de-camp to try an idea. Untethering his mare, Haji whipped her hindquarters with an elm switch and shouted, "Away!" The mare trotted off, leading Haji and the aide-de-camp's scout unerringly back to the place she had last seen her colt, at the border of the Country of Youth.

Safe, rested and warm in his palace, the Emperor summoned Haji to his gem-encrusted throne-room. The ruler asked his young subject how he had known the trick with the mare and the slaughtered colt. Haji looked the Emperor in the eye and said, "My grandmother told me, Your Majesty." The Emperor wanted to meet this wise woman. Haji replied, "That's a little difficult, Your Majesty. When she reached her sixtieth birthday, I persuaded her to go into hiding in the forest." Uproar broke out and Haji found a knife at his throat. The scandalized Emperor asked if Haji were not afraid for his life, following his confession. "I *am* afraid, Your Majesty," replied Haji, "but fear or no fear, how could I alter one word? Unless we respect our old people and listen to their wisdom, we damage ourselves and our future more than ten thousand bandits ever could." The Emperor was silent for a long time. His courtiers awaited his judgment. Haji, calmly, awaited his fate.

"What were the Emperor's words?" teased my old, wrinkled aunt, as she worked her loom, *click-clacketty, click-clacketty, click-clacketty.* "Work it out yourself, you young sappy idiot. I'm still here, with a few winters in me yet, aren't I? Look about you: hasn't the Country of Youth become the Country of All Ages?"

ARZÈSTULA

by Wu Ming 1

I. *The road from Parasacco to Medelana, November 16*

A persistent dream. I haven't finished my thesis, but continue to collect personal reminiscences from ancient parish priests and *basapilét*, bigoted old peasant women dressed in black. With my tape recorder as my constant companion, minor roads take me up to little gravel paths and from there onto muddy little tracks that lead from one cottage to another. I return to Ferrara with a rucksack full of unconnected stories, of a time when the missal was still in Latin, the priest stood with his back to you, and the chalice of wine was offered up *pro vobis et pro multis effendetur*, for the remission of sins (yours and those of others).

In the dream, I am twenty-five years old and I have to get a move on, stop "waffling." The deadline is just round the corner and my supervisor is getting impatient.

—Will you just make your mind up what it is you want to do! You've interviewed a hundred people, you must have some idea by now what to write about. You've read Portelli's book, you've read the one by Bermani *and* Montaldi's. What are your thoughts on memory as a source for history? Have you drafted an outline? Have you drawn all the appropriate comparisons?

A recurring dream. Each time I find myself at the bottom of a valley shrouded in mist, as intrepid as the first historian on Earth—she who tells the mother of all stories—and I discover that some other character has passed through before me, the interviewee is exhausted, she has talked for hours and can't take any more.

—You could've come to some agreement, *ragazòla*, if you'd both come at the same time I could've said all this stuff just the once . . . I talked about when I went to St. Peter's, about the pope who came to Consandolo . . . *Adès a son stufa, a voi andar a lèt.* I'm fed up now and just wanna go to bed.

Come to some agreement! It sounds easy, but I don't know who this creature who precedes me is. I only discover (I later discover) who it is in another dream but the dreams themselves are separate, watertight episodes. What I learn in one dream doesn't flow into the next.

But then, dreams are not the real world. No pope has ever been to Consandolo.

I have to rediscover, every single time, that the Writer always precedes me.

I wake up with a start, in the freezing cold. The word that pops into my head is in dialect: *Ingrottita.*

Ingrottita? Ingrottirsi, in the infinitive form. This verb doesn't exist in Italian. *Ingrutìras*, meaning: your body stiffening up in the freezing cold, as you lie curled up in your sleeping bag.

It's like a tiny explosion, a word reaching me from my childhood, seeping into my head. The language of my mother reaching out to me.

Here I am again, *sui mont ad Parasac*, on the mountains at Parasacco.

The mountains at Parasacco don't really exist. There's no high ground at Parasacco. No high ground anywhere nearby. Even before the Crisis the lowlands of the Po Basin were very low-lying indeed, a bowl of fog in a gray landscape. The "mountains" of Parasacco are two little bumps, mounds covered in weeds, in what was once a private courtyard. The expression is just an old witticism, a cliché from before the Crisis.

—Where did you go on holiday? asks one chap.

—*Sui mont ad Parasac!* replies the other, by which he means nowhere.

Peasant sarcasm.

Parasacco was a village of few houses, on a bend in the road that wound its way through clumps of trees to the south of Via Rossonia, just before the turning to Medelana. Via Rossonia went all the way to the Abbazia di Pomposa. Travelers on foot, however, would walk down to the *comune* of Ostellato, admiring on the way the bleak landscape with its network of access paths across the marshlands.

Medelana, already a ghost hamlet at the end of the last century, was now little more than a fleck of gray-green spittle on the horizon. When I was a young girl, *andar a Madlana*—to go to Medelana—meant going to watch porno films. There was a cinema in Medelana that my schoolmates used to go to even when they were under age. Sad little group pilgrimages. Still images projected onto a sheet, one after the other in sequence to create the illusion of movement: cock in, cock out, cock in, cock out, a little squirt and then it started all over again. Then the cinema closed down. Every now and then they reopened it for a bingo night, though less and less frequently, and in the end it was shut down completely.

Not far away was the defunct factory that used to produce the moulds for decoys—for hunting. Plastic ducks. The main wall collapsed, the rain ruined the large containers and the web-footed imitations escaped—so, plastic ducks on the San Nicolò canal, ducks on the branch of the Po at Volano. In my day, this part of the river was not as high or as wide. After the Crisis it rose by at least a yard and became wider. Now it really is a major river.

There it goes, the invincible armada of ducks on its way to the sea. Who knows where the ones that don't get stuck in the reed beds will end up? Maybe, a hundred years from now, they'll reach the *Grande Macchia*, the Big Dump, a vortex of rubbish that floats around in the Pacific and sooner or later picks up every bit of plastic that ends up in the water. I picture the *Macchia* in the sun: a calm, aromatic expanse. Sun-kissed. Photodegrading.

Ducks, here I come. My eagerness to be on the move is growing, *com al canarìn d'Alvo*—like Alvo's canary.

It's unbelievable, the things that come back to me! A story from before I was born: someone had sold a duckling to a chap called Alvo, pretending that it was a canary. Alvo put it in a cage and the "canary" grew and grew until . . . and that's the origin of the expression: *at crési com al canarìn d'Alvo*––"you've grown like Alvo's canary," people said to their grand-children between one visit and the next, or to preteens during the summers when their physical development would spurt. But I digress.

I wake up with a start, in the freezing cold. A pale light embraces the world, mist rising from the pools and large ponds that once were fields, just like the mist when I was a girl. To the northeast a jagged strip of land stretches out in front of me. The main highway to Porto Garibaldi. What's left of it.

I'm looking for my childhood home.

A few days ago, when I went into Ferrara, I found a copy of an old dictionary. Yellow scrunched-up pages covered in mildew. Luigi Ferri's *Ferrarese–Italian Dictionary*, 1889. I read it during my pilgrimage, entry by entry, page after page, camped out under ancient overpasses, sitting on my rolled-up sleeping bag, my legs aching after trudging thousands of steps through the mud.

What a mournful parade of extinct words! Dialect words used by my grandmothers, lost long before the Crisis.

Argùr
Zarabìgul
Arzèstula

147

. . . green lizard, ant-lion, great tit . . .

    Sciorzz
    Baciosa
    Capnégar

. . . glow-worm, curlew, blackcap . . .

Vague memories, sudden cranial jolts, a hesitant vibration of neurons.

    Aliévar
    Hare

By the time I could walk there were no longer any hares left in the fields behind our house. Exterminated, every last one of them. I didn't see a hare myself until I was nine, just its putrefied remains, maybe the last one from its world. Extermination: before the actual beings themselves existed, we didn't have the words for them. And now that these beings are returning, and I often hear curlews and on summer evenings I see glow-worms everywhere, the words *sciorzz* and *baciosa* are more dead than ever.

The re-flooding, slow but inexorable, of once reclaimed land is in full flow. The eastern part of the old province is, in parts, more than four yards below sea level, and the water refuses to budge; it wants to return to the places it was expelled from. The

Commission still has a degree of control, but elsewhere water pumps are no longer working and whole *comuni* have surrendered. Goodness knows what has happened to the Magoghe. It was the lowest inhabited place in Italy.

We took the land around us for granted. Few people stopped to think that every damn day somebody had to keep the water in check and pump it away so that our houses didn't flood. I offer up a prayer to the workers in the Consortium. I thank them for what they did, and I thank those who have stayed behind to keep watch. I thank them for their futile, Sisyphean efforts to keep above water land that sooner or later will inevitably surrender to the sea. Its salty waters are already rising, the coast is slowly drowning. At least, that's what travelers say. That's what the amateur radio operator from Porto Tolle says.

I think of you, guardian of the reclaimed land. I don't know who is paying you, or how or how much. I don't know what you think you will save or why it is important to you. I don't know what you dream about, but I do know that you are saving something, and I am your ally, your sister. I, like you, and you, like me, both look for a future in the past.

Today, anyway, the waters of the canal are still. For the last week the sky has spared us; it threatens and is sad, but it doesn't weep.

Little of my childhood home is left standing: split in two by climbing plants, tilting towards the north because of the pine tree that fell onto it. And it's so small . . . When I was *cìrula*, a little girl, it encircled me like a palace. In winter it kept us warm. Outside the snow covered the ground and under its mantle memories of games played in the sunshine were buried underground like spring bulbs.

April sped by, its clouds not yet emptied, and summer surprised us with late-falling showers of rain; we would shelter under the entrances to the haylofts, many of which had already been abandoned. On dry days, we lay in the sun, drank lemonade, flirted, chattering about nothing. But that chatter was *us*, who we were.

Now the house is so poky, perhaps because I'm practically on stilts. It feels like there's nine inches of mud on the soles of my boots.

The gods were kind to mother and father. They passed away before the Crisis and are spared the sight of all of this devastation today.

The sun is already low in the sky. I don't want to go in. I won't be strong enough.

Something furry slips through a gap in the crumbling walls. It's a rat. No, it's a ferret. A ferret slips away without looking at me and disappears into the bushes. It must be a descendant of pets that turned feral, the owners not having been able to get them sterilized in time.

The Crisis arrived before the vet did.

I can't sleep. I am reading. It's nearly dawn but I am reading. The light from the bonfire makes the letters tremble on the page.

Arzèstula

A *bissabuò*
Snèstnar
Barbagùl

. . . zigzagging, sideways, wattles . . .

Pinguèl
Budlòz
Rugnir

. . . palate, umbilical chord, to neigh . . .

The ruins of a language are heart-wrenching. Every word that dies out is a house that gives up, sags and sinks, becomes buried in the sand.

These words were inhabited, human beings filled them with life and stories.

When you look at the ruins of a house they help you imagine what the home was like. You hear footsteps, the sound of little children at play, voices that come and go . . . But you can't inhabit the ruins in the same way that you inhabit a home. The home no longer exists.

I look up from my book and for a long time I search for the Pleiades, but I can't find them.

It's my last day here. Tomorrow I am going back to the southwest.

*II. San Vito, November 22, on my
way to Bologna once again.*

Am ambushed by a solitary marauder, hidden among the
bushes surrounding the parish church of San Vito. An inch
further to the left and he would have broken my nose, but I
was already moving back and his stick just struck me a glancing
blow. He put his full force behind it and lost his balance. I saw
him fall badly and hit his elbow on a stone.

—Ouch! he exclaimed, just like in the comics you find rotting
away in the ditches. Putrefied stories. I also found bundles of
torn euros, not that they'd be any use. Not here, anyway.

He has picked himself up. Now he's staring at me with curi-
osity. He is thin (who isn't?). He has green eyes and mousy
hair. The rags he's wearing remind me of something. I recognize them: the uniform and greatcoat of the carabinieri.

—You're not from around here, you can tell.

—How? I was born here, though I live miles away now.

When I use the feminine conjugation of the verb "born," he
lights up.

—Wow, you're a woman! I'd never have guessed!

I lift my hood and pull down my scarf. He can see that I am
middle-aged. He can see my wrinkles and his smile fades but
doesn't disappear altogether.

—Where do you live now? What have you come back for?

—I could say that that's *my* business, I reply, but lightly, with
no hostility in my voice.

He sniggers.

—And you would be well within your rights. And what if I ask you what your name is? Any name will do.

He's welcome to my name. He offers me his hand and I shake it. His hand is cold.

—I'm Matteo, he says.

—Are you a marauder, Matteo?

—*Moché, moché!* You must be joking, I thought *you* were the marauder! Because I'd never seen you before.

—I'm just a passerby.

—Aren't you afraid, traveling on your own?

—Like everybody else. No more, no less. But what were you up to in the bushes?

—I was emptying my bowels, he replies straightaway. Actually, I hadn't yet started. And now it's gone back up. Still, it'll come back down.

And he laughs again, this time more loudly.

We are silent for a while. We look about us. The plane trees that line Via Ferrara, which is no longer tarmacked, are enormous. No one prunes anymore. Everywhere huge branches intertwine, making a roof overhead. The old trunk road is like a tunnel. Underneath, somebody is obviously still pulling up the weeds, moving fallen branches, filling in the biggest holes in the road. The road is stony but passable.

—While I'm at it, can I ask you something else? I promise you it won't piss you off, ok?

—I nod in agreement.

—*Bon.* What's the government doing? Does it still exist where you are?

153

—No. There's a skeleton government, but it's still in the South.

—That's what I imagined. Here only the Commission shows up. The ex-carabiniere who I thought was a bandit shrugs his shoulders. They help us, if you can call it that. Goodness knows why.

—They do it in exchange for the services provided by the government. Do you sleep inside the church? I ask him.

—My feet decide where I sleep. And what does the government do, exactly?

—It patrols the coastlands, the borders with Europe. The Ionian Sea, the Tyrrhenian Sea . . . It arrests and drives out illegal immigrants.

—Kills them, more like. I know how these things work, I was part of the system.

And at this point a pause would be good, a moment to think, but the man goes straight on.

—It's crazy, are there really still people who want to come to this bog? he says.

—Some parts of Italy are still functioning okay, and in any case it's worse in Africa. But, you know, lots of them don't come here to stay. It's more that Italy is the weak link. They arrive here, if they are able to, and move north, if they are able to. They move north into Europe.

—To do what? Is there any work still?

—I think so, something like that.

Then it's my turn to ask him a question.

—How often does the Commission show up? I've been crossing the province for days and I've yet to see a single official.

—It depends. They come by helicopter. They're the only people who have fuel. Some of them look Chinese.

By helicopter? I've seen a few gliders and hang gliders recently. I've seen some hot-air balloons and even an airship, but I've never ever seen any helicopters. And given the noise they make, surely I'd have noticed them.

Maybe I spoke my thoughts out loud because Matteo insists.

—They do come, they do. They land in the village squares, hand out rations, hold meetings with the local councilors——

—Local councilors? Have elections started up again?

—Well, in a manner of speaking . . . The commissioners didn't want them to, but people organize themselves. As I am well aware, because I'm a councilor, too.

—Oh, yes? Where?

—Gambulaga.

—It wasn't a local council in my time.

—Everything changes. Especially the times. Have you got anything to eat?

In my rucksack I have the frogs I caught yesterday. There's a lot of them. I cook them on a spit, the meat tasteless but crunchy. And I have a bunch of wild radicchio. Matteo shows me a purple water-bottle.

—There's something to drink, too, he says. Clean water, purified with alum given out by the Commission.

And so we eat together, at the edge of the little wood behind the church.

—It's windy, I say. Why don't we go inside the church?

—It's dangerous in there. God's in there. Here we're safe.

I accept his answer, without asking for further explanations.

—Are you going back home? Matteo asks.

The local councilor who had been about to kill me wants to talk.

—Yes. Near Bologna. Casalecchio.

—What, all the way to Casalecchio on foot?

—There's still some transport available when you get past Ferrara. And lots of horses. I'll hitch a lift, like I did to get here. I saw some hot-air balloons tethered in a field. If they can be used, that would be even better.

—Don't people still shoot at the balloons?

—I don't think so. That only happened in the early days.

—And have you got any money to pay for the ride?

—Money's not much use any more. The Commission changes money into vouchers, and I've got a few.

For a while we concentrate on our food, our jaws working, tongues mixing it up, our gastric juices getting to work.

—Did you come through Ferrara?

The dream from a few nights ago. A city—it feels unreal. On a dark foggy winter's morning a river of people flows over the city walls, and there are truly a lot of them, a greater number than all of history's dead combined. They look down at their feet and every now and then they sigh. They charge over the Montagnone and down Via Alfonso d'Este, all the way to where the branch of the River Po at Volano flows under the bridge. I see someone I used to know and call out to him.

—Rizzi! You once stood with me in front of the war memorial in Udine. The body that you buried in the garden has begun to sprout. What do you think, will it bloom this year? Or has the big freeze destroyed the garden? Please be careful, keep the dog away. It digs up the soil and it likes men!

—Did you come through Ferrara? I've not been there for eight years and it's only twelve miles away.

—Yes, but I didn't stop. People told me it was dangerous.

—The last time I was there—Matteo is talking again—the Crisis was very recent. You could still find petrol on the black market and I went on my moped to look at the petro-chemical plant. It was swarming with officials from the Commission. You can imagine, what with all those toxic substances about to leak out and kill everything . . . The various parts of the plant were holding up well and I've heard that they're still standing firm. They'd already stopped producing some things before the Crisis and at that time a large number of silos, full of ammonia or whatever, went missing. Carted away, goodness knows where.

—Africa, I reckon.

—Expect so, he says, but adds nothing.

A few minutes of peaceful silence follow. Tiredness flows out of my body through my pores, my muscles discharge toxins, and even my mind is restored. My eyesight becomes keener and my ears stop buzzing. My lunch companion glances up at me, but I am the first to start up the conversation again.

—You said that people around here are organizing themselves. Tell me: what does a local council do?

He snorts.

—Hah! Not much. It decides how to distribute aid, rounds up volunteers to pull up weeds in the fields. It writes to the relatives of the dead . . . I used to be a carabiniere. You can tell, can't you? When the Crisis happened I was in Cosenza. In order to get back home I took a train like the ones you used to see in documentaries, you know, like in India, with people even sitting on the roof. It took me two days. It kept stopping in little villages I'd never even heard of . . . And you, what kind of work did you do?

My other recurring dream. I am twenty-eight years old, I am writing my first novel. It is about the lives of a group of young seminarists at the time of the Second Vatican Council: forbidden loves, theological arguments, squabbles and disagreements, an unforeseen death. They come from peasant families—devout but not overly so—and I have to try and depict a background of popular religious sentiment. I draw on the "anthropology" of the changes taking place at that time. In fact, I am killing two birds with one stone because I'm using material from my thesis. Nothing ever gets thrown away.

In the dream, goodness knows why, I meet people I had interviewed three years earlier. They are so pleased to see me, they tell me everything, all over again, from the beginning. I say goodbye to them feeling very satisfied, aware that it will be a good book. Then I discover that all the time, *She* is hobbling along behind me: the Historian. *She* is left behind in a cloud of dust, but still recognizably me: twenty-five years old and behind with my thesis. I turn up late and nobody wants to talk to me because *I have already been there before.*

—. . . work did you do?

—I was a writer, I reply to Matteo.

—A writer? What sort of thing did you write?

—Novels. At least that's what people called them.

—Novels. And he pauses to think. I used to read them too, but I don't think I read any by women. I used to read detective stories and stuff like that.

—Yes, before the Crisis they were very popular. But who'd want to read books like that these days?

—That's true. So now what do you do?

Words precede thought.

—I'm still a writer, in a way, but I don't write any more.

—What a strange thing to say. What do you mean?

—That these days I don't write: *I see.*

—I don't follow.

—The future. I see the future.

A pause.

—So, you're . . . What's it called? . . . A soothsayer?

—Don't know if that's the right word.

—But you see the future. Is that why you managed to dodge my cudgel? So can you tell what's in store for us?

—No. No to both your questions. I'm not interested in that kind of insignificant future.

—*Insignificant!* You say these things but I don't know what you mean. And what a funny phrase to use, "interested in" . . . I haven't heard that for a long time.

—Yes, I'm *interested in* something. In the future perfect. The one that comes after the insignificant future. I see it and I tell people about it.

—What people?

—I have a family, a very large one. I tell the future perfect, we see it together, and we all feel better. They depend on me and I'm going back to them.

—Fair enough. So, you . . . erm . . . took a holiday. I know that's not the right word. I mean that you needed to distance yourself a bit, to see the place where you were born. Is that right?

The simple thing that is difficult to say.

—Yes. That's absolutely right. Then, without preamble, I add, Do you remember how to say "great tit" in the Ferrarese dialect?

Matteo doesn't seem surprised by this reference to a local bird. He concentrates, not speaking. He looks up at the branches of the trees and the roof of the church. He stands up, takes a sip from his water-bottle and walks around slowly. Very slowly. I am no longer there, he's lost in childhood memories. Not even his, probably: his mother's. His grandmother's and even further back than that. Finally he stops and opens his eyes wide. He points his right index finger—rigid and straight as a flagpole—toward the sky. He turns toward me and exclaims:

—*Arzèstula!* But why did you ask me that? Is it something to do with the future perfect?

And at that very moment we hear it, a female great tit, and we can see it, too, on the branch of a leafless ash tree behind the parish church. Yellow and black, perfectly formed, a heart-breaking marvel of Evolution. We are left open-mouthed, here, now.

III. From the Parco della Chiusa to the ex-motorway café, the Cantagallo, at Casalecchio sul Reno, November 26–27

There are a lot of fallen trees and their rotten trunks block the paths, making the ground very slippery. The soles of my boots are muddy and I fall, two, three times, and when I get up again I sink up to my ankles in mud. I'm forced to make little detours to clean the soles of my boots on stones and dry twigs. On my right, a powerful river, the Reno, flows by; I can't see it but I can hear its roar, beyond this strip of woodland that lines one of its deep banks, beyond the screen of alders and willows and the tangle of reed beds.

I finally reach the bridge, a small steel walkway that is just as I had left it. I stride on to it, and then there it is, the river, and I'm overcome; the river is stereotypically blue, just as it's supposed to be, but different from everything else. It flows down from the Apennines and crosses the great plain, toward me and the places that I am leaving behind.

On the other side, the old gravel heaps belonging to the SAPABA quarry await me; now they are just hills, nothing more, covered in plants so green they hurt my eyes. But I leave them behind and quicken my pace. A sudden frenzy moves my legs along. Off with my hood, off with my scarf, I'm nearly home, home! Once upon a time there was a camp of nomads here, but nowadays the whole of Italy is one big camp of nomads. And maybe a good part of the world, too. But I am home. I turn right, I step onto one last pathway and there it is. The Cantagallo Café.

My family welcomes me joyfully. I've been gone forty days, visiting my old haunts, back to my origins, clearing my mind and my body. For weeks I had been suffering from visual disturbances, caused by waves of heat, hot flushes, which started deep inside me and pervaded my whole body. I felt them in my chest, I felt them on my neck. I turned up at the ritual tired out after sleepless nights, troubled by a burning sensation whenever I went for a pee and the friction of my exploratory fingertips on dry mucosa, everything setting me on edge. At times I would burst into tears during the storytelling, upsetting the others, bringing the whole ritual to a halt. Entering into this new stage of life stopped me from functioning properly. The menopause forced me to face my insignificant personal future, to ask myself what would become of me and my place in the world. It was a final farewell to fertility: an unexpected blow even for me. I had always been infertile because of some peculiarity of my womb. I had to stop, withdraw, withdraw and rethink everything, remember everything, far away from this place, which belongs to a different stage. I had to shake up my body, put it to the test.

—Tonight, we are going to celebrate! Eat, drink and make love! Nita announces.

It's lovely to see her again. Forty days ago, when she said goodbye to me her voice was cracked and unhappy. Now it rings out like the telephone used to when I was a child. Nita is twenty-five years old, and I'm about to turn fifty-two. We are the vice and the versa. While I was away, I know she was the one who led the ritual, who saw, who started the storytelling. I am confident she has worked well. I have taught her a lot of what I know.

A lot, yes, but not everything. There are a lot of things I do unconsciously, without thinking, so I can't teach them.

I *see*. Much more than that, I couldn't say.

I am the clairvoyant from the Cantagallo Café, the woman who leads this family, who sees and narrates distant futures. I went through my personal crisis at the time of *the* Crisis, and I have returned to where I feel better, to live with those I love, to grow old with those I love, and one day to die with those I love by my side.

Here they are, laughing, hugging and kissing me. I find the hugs from those who only have one limb very moving. They are off-balance, they remind me of the dancers in *Zorba the Greek*.

There they are, my little ones, with their illnesses, their strengths, their hopes.

I greet Antioco, who suffers from Capgras syndrome. If he looked me in the face he would not recognize me. I would look like some stranger who resembles me, a dummy made of flesh with my features. In order to love me, *in order to love anyone*, he has to close his eyes, because a person's voice, *that* always stays true. He lowers his eyelids and smiles at me.

I greet Ileana, who suffers from Fregoli syndrome. She doesn't look at me either, she moves, eyes wet with tears, towards Nita; overwhelmed by emotion, she hugs her and greets her . . . calling her by my name. Nita doesn't correct her, nor do I. It's fine as it is.

I greet Ezio, who is nearly blind but doesn't know it, he refuses to know it. He suffers from Anton syndrome. He fixes his sightless gaze on my nose. My face is maybe just a pale spot, and maybe not even that, but Ezio is happy to see me again and he says—You look radiant. Your trip has really done you good!

I greet Demetra, Tiziano and Lizbet, who don't suffer from any syndrome. I greet Edo, Yassin, Pablo and Natzuko. I greet the children who cling to my legs. I greet the dogs and goats. In my thoughts I greet every animal and every plant in our orbit, in this world of splendid refugees, this nation gathered together in an old motorway café, above a deserted motorway, where the rare sight of a passing motor vehicle is a source of wonderment. This café that can still function as such, because we give sustenance and shelter to travelers, because we were all travelers before coming here from far and wide. Rejects. Rejects who every morning grab hold of the future by its tail to be pulled at speed out of the present, happy to be here, ready to face the day, to raise animals and cultivate crops, to teach and educate, to go off to explore and return to tell the story.

✳   ✳   ✳

The middle of the night, a curved sliver of a moon and not a cloud in the sky. I stare down through a long window at the A1 motorway. Every stone, every slab, every nail and screw of the Cantagallo Café could tell millions of stories.

Here, in 1971, the workers went on a wildcat strike so that they wouldn't have to fill up the car belonging to Giorgio Almirante—a politician back then—or serve him coffee. A popular song, maybe one of the last ones, was written about it, and I can still remember the words:

Arriving at the Cantagallo, he finds a nice place to eat,
Thank goodness, Almirante thought: at least we're in for a
  treat.
Everybody out, arms folded, Almirante pleads in vain.
No lunch for black shirts, hungry they must remain.

Nowadays it seems like a myth from the Bronze Age.
—Who was Al Mirante? Nita asked me one summer's afternoon.
—He was the leader of the fascists.
—And who were the *fascists*?
It was here, on New Year's Eve 2002, that the first receipt was issued in the new currency, the euro. It was in the papers. The holder of this record was called Lorenzo. His purchase: a packet of chewing gum full of aspartame. Memento of the Second Age of Cancer.
—What was 'spartame? Pablo asked one autumn evening.
—Something sweet that was very harmful to people's health, but everybody ate and drank it.

165

—Why, if it was harmful?

It was here, in 2006, that a lorry driver shouted that he was wearing a belt packed with explosives, causing panic in the restaurant. He demanded that the police shoot him, otherwise he would blow the building up. He wanted to be killed. The Cantagallo was evacuated and the authorities closed the A1 between Casalecchio and Sasso Marconi. There was chaos everywhere. After an hour of negotiations, the police convinced the man to surrender. He had a cushion hidden under his coat and the detonator wire was a mobile phone charger. He said he had problems at work, he was being exploited and his family was falling apart.

Mine isn't. After the party, music is still playing in some of the rooms. A few people are wandering around, talking to each other, others are snoring, reassured, clinging to each other in their sleeping bags.

I go up onto the roof, where we have built a kind of telescope. It's a perfect night for looking at the stars. Nights like this are less rare than they once were; thanks to the Crisis, the vault of heaven is clear, you no longer feel as if you are at the bottom of a glass of fluorescent barley water.

I don't touch the telescope. With the naked eye you can see the mass of the Pleiades, the daughters of Atlas and Pleione.

When you next lose yourself between water and land, stare up at the night sky, examine it, searching for secrets. Deepest space will be there to draw you in, a never-ending, tantalizing emptiness.

Afterwards, you will lower your gaze, your spirit cheered, aware of your center of gravity.

I have traveled through the womb of the earth, I have witnessed the breaking of its waters and I am reborn.

Back in the world, back in my place.

For me.

And for the others.

IV. *The former motorway café, the Cantagallo,* *Casalecchio sul Reno, December 1*

Two hours from now it will be dawn. We are getting ready to welcome it.

From the roof of the motorway café, from a hundred mouths, the vapor from our breath rises up.

Venus, the light-giving morning star, the only planet with a woman's name, is visible in the east. I can see it out of the corner of my right eye.

Facing north, eyes closed, tongues pressing against our palates, we breathe through our noses. Teeth mustn't touch.

Hands relaxed over our abdomens, between the umbilical cord and the pubis.

Those who only have one hand use them both anyway.

We imagine that we are holding a sphere, a black sphere, we test its weight. Our lungs are full. Now we breathe out and the sphere starts to turn anticlockwise, caressing the palms of our hands and our fingertips. We feel its movement, we savor it, we sense the slight friction of its smooth surface. With every exhalation, the rotation quickens, and when we breathe in it begins to slow down. This is repeated eighteen times.

From now on, with every exhalation the sphere becomes bigger until it enters our abdomens, right up to where it can caress our kidneys. We breathe in, the sphere slows down and returns to the same size as before, contained within the bounds of our circle of hands.

This is repeated ninety, one hundred and eighty times. Our hands are on fire.

Now, while the sphere expands and contracts, we imagine that we too are getting bigger, with every exhalation we are taller and taller. Beside us, level with our eyes, we see the moon.

We fix our gaze on the North Star. Polaris, the last star in the Little Bear. Let's look at it: its light travels in the void for more than four hundred years before it reaches our eyes and activates our photoreceptors.

The light that we now see was emitted when the Inquisition was trying Galileo—the scholar who bequeathed us our telescope.

The light that we now see was emitted while building on the Taj Mahal—a distant palace, much older than the Cantagallo—was just beginning.

The light that we now see was emitted nearly thirteen billion seconds ago.

We hold our breath for thirteen seconds.

We multiply by one thousand the time we hold our breath.

We multiply the result by one thousand.

This is one thousandth of the time it takes for the light from Polaris to reach us.

We cannot see the light that it emits now. The people who come after us, in four centuries' time, will see it.

Now look at the North Star, look at it with new eyes.

One day, in twelve thousand years' time, Polaris will be replaced and at that point in the sky we shall see Vega.

Let's say goodbye to Polaris and thank it. It has done good work.

Let's welcome Vega.

Now we look down, towards the planet. Down, towards the planet, twelve thousand years hence.

Where once upon a time the city of Bologna rose up, everything is now one huge wood.

The sphere enters our abdomens for the last time. As it does, it becomes smaller and smaller until it disappears. We place our hands just below our abdomens and massage ourselves in an anticlockwise direction.

We imagine ourselves becoming smaller, too. With every exhalation we become shorter and shorter until we return to earth.

The Cantagallo is no longer there. In its place, just a grassy clearing. Around us only trees.

We are not alone. There are other humans around us. They move without bumping into us even though they don't see us.

We have advanced twelve thousand years minus two hours. Again it's two hours until dawn. These humans, our descendants, face north and get ready to welcome it. Their gaze seeks out and finds Vega, the North Star. In their hands the sphere expands and contracts. In their minds, their heads are already above our atmosphere. They can touch the moon.

One day, in thirteen thousand years' time, Vega will be replaced at that point in the sky and in its place humans will see Polaris again.

These descendants of ours say goodbye to Vega and thank it. It has done good work. They welcome back Polaris, and so do we.

Now, from on high they look down, towards the planet, towards us, but they do not see us.

They see what it will be like in thirteen thousand years' time.

Soon they will descend and by their side their descendants will look north.

And so on, along the chain of millennia, through ice ages and thaws, the rise and fall of civilizations, until they witness the night of the last ritual.

Now we turn back, we return here, to the Cantagallo. Each exhalation takes us back a thousand years.

The sun begins to rise. A day's work awaits us, our hands are full of energy.

Let's get to work.

THE TAMARISK HUNTER

by Paolo Bacigalupi

A big tamarisk can suck 73,000 gallons of river water a year. For $2.88 a day, plus water bounty, Lolo rips tamarisk all winter long.

Ten years ago, it was a good living. Back then, tamarisk shouldered up against every riverbank in the Colorado River Basin, along with cottonwoods, Russian olives, and elms. Ten years ago, towns like Grand Junction and Moab thought they could still squeeze life from a river.

Lolo stands on the edge of a canyon, Maggie the camel his only companion. He stares down into the deeps. It's an hour's scramble to the bottom. He ties Maggie to a juniper and starts down, boot-skiing a gully. A few blades of green grass sprout neon around him, piercing juniper-tagged snow clods. In the late winter, there is just a beginning surge of water down in the deeps; the ice is off the river edges. Up high, the mountains still wear their ragged snow mantles. Lolo smears through mud and

171

hits a channel of scree, sliding and scattering rocks. His jugs of tamarisk poison gurgle and slosh on his back. His shovel and rockbar snag on occasional junipers as he skids by. It will be a long hike out. But then, that's what makes this patch so perfect. It's a long way down, and the riverbanks are largely hidden.

It's a living; where other people have dried out and blown away, he has remained: a tamarisk hunter, a water tick, a stubborn bit of weed. Everyone else has been blown off the land as surely as dandelion seeds, set free to fly south or east, or most of all north where watersheds sometimes still run deep and where even if there are no more lush ferns or deep cold fish runs, at least there is still water for people.

Eventually, Lolo reaches the canyon bottom. Down in the cold shadows, his breath steams.

He pulls out a digital camera and starts shooting his proof. The Bureau of Reclamation has gotten uptight about proof. They want different angles on the offending tamarisk, they want each one photographed before and after, the whole process documented, GPS'd, and uploaded directly by the camera. They want it done on-site. And then they still sometimes come out to spot check before they calibrate his headgate for water bounty.

But all their due diligence can't protect them from the likes of Lolo. Lolo has found the secret to eternal life as a tamarisk hunter. Unknown to the Interior Department and its BuRec subsidiary, he has been seeding new patches of tamarisk, encouraging vigorous brushy groves in previously cleared areas. He has hauled and planted healthy root balls up and down the river system in strategically hidden and inaccessible corridors, all in a bid for security against the swarms of other tamarisk hunters that scour these same tributaries. Lolo is crafty. Stands like this one, a quarter-mile long and thick with salt-laden tamarisk, are his insurance policy.

Documentation finished, he unstraps a folding saw, along with his rockbar and shovel, and sets his poison jugs on the dead salt bank. He starts cutting, slicing into the roots of the tamarisk, pausing every thirty seconds to spread Garlon 4 on the cuts, poisoning the tamarisk wounds faster than they can heal. But some of the best tamarisk, the most vigorous, he uproots and sets aside, for later use.

$2.88 a day, plus water bounty.

It takes Maggie's rolling bleating camel stride a week to make it back to Lolo's homestead. They follow the river, occasionally climbing above it onto cold mesas or wandering off into the open desert in a bid to avoid the skeleton sprawl of emptied towns. Guardie choppers buzz up and down the river like swarms of angry yellowjackets, hunting for porto-pumpers and wildcat diversions. They rush overhead in a wash of beaten air and gleaming National Guard logos. Lolo remembers a time when the guardies traded potshots with people down on the river banks, tracer-fire and machine-gun chatter echoing in the canyons. He remembers the glorious hiss and arc of a Stinger missile as it flashed across redrock desert and blue sky and burned a chopper where it hovered.

But that's long in the past. Now, guardie patrols skim up the river unmolested.

Lolo tops another mesa and stares down at the familiar landscape of an eviscerated town, its curving streets and subdivision cul-de-sacs all sitting silent in the sun. At the very edge of the empty town, one-acre ranchettes and snazzy five-thousand-square-foot houses with dead-stick trees and dust-hill landscaping fringe a brown tumbleweed golf course. The sandtraps don't even show any more.

When California put its first calls on the river, no one really worried. A couple of towns went begging for water. Some idiot newcomers with bad water rights stopped grazing their horses, and that was it. A few years later, people started showering real fast. And a few after that, they showered once a week. And then people started using the buckets. By then, everyone had stopped joking about how "hot" it was. It didn't really matter how "hot" it was. The problem wasn't lack of water or an excess of heat, not really. The problem was that 4.4 million acre-feet of water were supposed to go down the river to California. There was water; they just couldn't touch it.

They were supposed to stand there like dumb monkeys and watch it flow on by.

"Lolo?"

The voice catches him by surprise. Maggie startles and groans and lunges for the mesa edge before Lolo can rein her around. The camel's great padded feet scuffle dust and Lolo flails for his shotgun where it nestles in a scabbard at the camel's side. He forces Maggie to turn, shotgun half-drawn, holding barely to his seat and swearing.

A familiar face, tucked amongst juniper tangle.

"Goddammit!" Lolo lets the shotgun drop back into its scabbard. "Jesus Christ, Travis. You scared the hell out of me."

Travis grins. He emerges from amongst the junipers' silver bark rags, one hand on his gray fedora, the other on the reins as he guides his mule out of the trees. "Surprised?"

"I could've shot you!"

"Don't be so jittery. There's no one out here 'cept us water ticks."

"That's what I thought the last time I went shopping down there. I had a whole set of new dishes for Annie and I broke them all when I ran into an ultralight parked right in the middle of the main drag."

"Meth flyers?"

"Beats the hell out of me. I didn't stick around to ask."

"Shit. I'll bet they were as surprised as you were."

"They almost killed me."

"I guess they didn't."

Lolo shakes his head and swears again, this time without anger. Despite the ambush, he's happy to run into Travis. It's lonely country, and Lolo's been out long enough to notice the silence of talking to Maggie. They trade ritual sips of water from their canteens and make camp together. They swap stories about BuRec and avoid discussing where they've been ripping tamarisk and enjoy the view of the empty town far below, with its serpentine streets and quiet houses and shining untouched river.

It isn't until the sun is setting and they've finished roasting a magpie that Lolo finally asks the question that's been on his mind ever since Travis's sun-baked face came out of the tangle. It goes against etiquette, but he can't help himself. He picks magpie out of his teeth and says, "I thought you were working downriver."

Travis glances sidelong at Lolo and in that one suspicious uncertain look, Lolo sees that Travis has hit a lean patch. He's not smart like Lolo. He hasn't been reseeding. He's got no insurance. He hasn't been thinking ahead about all the competition, and what the tamarisk endgame looks like, and now he's feeling the pinch. Lolo feels a twinge of pity. He likes Travis. A part of him wants to tell Travis the secret, but he stifles the urge. The stakes are too high. Water crimes are serious now, so serious Lolo hasn't even told his wife, Annie, for fear of what she'll say. Like all of the most shameful crimes, water theft is a private business, and at the scale Lolo works, forced labor on the Straw is the best punishment he can hope for.

Travis gets his hackles down over Lolo's invasion of his privacy and says, "I had a couple cows I was running up here, but I lost 'em. I think something got 'em."

"Long way to graze cows."

"Yeah, well, down my way even the sagebrush is dead. Big Daddy Drought's doing a real number on my patch." He pinches his lip, thoughtful. "Wish I could find those cows."

"They probably went down to the river."

Travis sighs. "Then the guardies probably got 'em."

"Probably shot 'em from a chopper and roasted 'em."

"Californians."

They both spit at the word. The sun continues to sink.

Shadows fall across the town's silent structures. The rooftops gleam red, a ruby cluster decorating the blue river necklace.

"You think there's any stands worth pulling down there?" Travis asks.

"You can go down and look. But I think I got it all last year. And someone had already been through before me, so I doubt much is coming up."

"Shit. Well, maybe I'll go shopping. Might as well get something out of this trip."

"There sure isn't anyone to stop you."

As if to emphasize the fact, the thud-thwap of a guardie chopper breaks the evening silence. The black-fly dot of its movement barely shows against the darkening sky. Soon it's out of sight and cricket chirps swallow the last evidence of its passing.

Travis laughs. "Remember when the guardies said they'd keep out looters? I saw them on TV with all their choppers and Humvees and them all saying they were going to protect everything until the situation improved." He laughs again. "You remember that? All of them driving up and down the streets?"

"I remember."

"Sometimes I wonder if we shouldn't have fought them more."

"Annie was in Lake Havasu City when they fought there. You saw what happened." Lolo shivers. "Anyway, there's not much to fight for once they blow up your water treatment plant. If nothing's coming out of your faucet, you might as well move on."

"Yeah, well, sometimes I think you still got to fight. Even if it's just for pride." Travis gestures at the town below, a shadow movement. "I remember when all that land down there was selling like hotcakes and they were building shit as fast as they could ship in the lumber. Shopping malls and parking lots and subdivisions, anywhere they could scrape a flat spot."

"We weren't calling it Big Daddy Drought, back then."

"Forty-five thousand people. And none of us had a clue. And I was a real estate agent." Travis laughs, a self-mocking sound that ends quickly. It sounds too much like self-pity for Lolo's taste. They're quiet again, looking down at the town wreckage.

"I think I might be heading north," Travis says finally.

Lolo glances over, surprised. Again he has the urge to let Travis in on his secret, but he stifles it. "And do what?"

"Pick fruit, maybe. Maybe something else. Anyway, there's water up there."

Lolo points down at the river. "There's water."

"Not for us." Travis pauses. "I got to level with you, Lolo. I went down to the Straw."

For a second, Lolo is confused by the non sequitur. The statement is too outrageous. And yet Travis's face is serious. "The Straw? No kidding? All the way there?"

"All the way there." He shrugs defensively. "I wasn't finding any tamarisk, anyway. And it didn't actually take that long. It's a lot closer than it used to be. A week out to the train tracks, and then I hopped a coal train, and rode it right to the inter-state, and then I hitched."

"What's it like out there?"

"Empty. A trucker told me that California and the Interior Department drew up all these plans to decide which cities they'd turn off when." He looks at Lolo significantly. "That was after Lake Havasu. They figured out they had to do it slow. They worked out some kind of formula: how many cities, how many people they could evaporate at a time without making too much unrest. Got advice from the Chinese, from when they were shutting down their old communist industries. Anyway, it looks like they're pretty much done with it. There's nothing moving out there except highway trucks and coal trains and a couple truck stops."

"And you saw the Straw?"

"Oh sure, I saw it. Out toward the border. Big old mother. So big you couldn't climb on top of it, flopped out on the desert like a damn silver snake. All the way to California." He spits reflexively. "They're spraying with concrete to keep water from seeping into the ground and they've got some kind of carbon-fiber stuff over the top to stop the evaporation. And the river just disappears inside. Nothing but an empty canyon below it. Bone-dry. And choppers and Humvees everywhere, like a damn hornet's nest. They wouldn't let me get any closer than a half mile on account of the eco-crazies trying to blow it up. They weren't nice about it, either."

"What did you expect?"

"I dunno. It sure depressed me, though: They work us out here and toss us a little water bounty and then all that water next year goes right down into that big old pipe. Some Californian's probably filling his swimming pool with last year's water bounty right now."

Cricket-song pulses in the darkness. Off in the distance, a pack of coyotes starts yipping. The two of them are quiet for a while. Finally, Lolo chucks his friend on the shoulder. "Hell, Travis, it's probably for the best. A desert's a stupid place to put a river, anyway."

Lolo's homestead runs across a couple acres of semi-alkaline soil, conveniently close to the river's edge. Annie is out in the field when he crests the low hills that overlook his patch. She waves, but keeps digging, planting for whatever water he can collect in bounty.

Lolo pauses, watching Annie work. Hot wind kicks up, carrying with it the scents of sage and clay. A dust devil swirls around Annie, whipping her bandana off her head. Lolo smiles as she snags it; she sees him still watching her and waves at him to quit loafing.

He grins to himself and starts Maggie down the hill, but he doesn't stop watching Annie work. He's grateful for her. Grateful that every time he comes back from tamarisk hunting she is still here. She's steady. Steadier than the people like Travis who give up when times get dry. Steadier than anyone Lolo knows, really. And if she has nightmares sometimes, and can't stand being in towns or crowds and wakes up in the middle of the night calling out for family she'll never see again, well, then it's all the more reason to seed more tamarisk and make sure they never get pushed off their patch like she was pushed.

Lolo gets Maggie to kneel down so he can dismount, then leads her over to a water trough, half-full of slime and water skippers. He gets a bucket and heads for the river while Maggie groans and complains behind him. The patch used to have a well and running water, but like everyone else, they lost their pumping rights and BuRec stuffed the well with Quickcrete when the water table dropped below the Minimum Allowable Reserve. Now he and Annie steal buckets from the river, or, when the Interior Department isn't watching, they jump up and down on a footpump and dump water into a hidden underground cistern he built when the Resource Conservation and Allowable Use Guidelines went into effect.

Annie calls the guidelines "RaCAUG" and it sounds like she's hawking spit when she says it, but even with their filled-in well, they're lucky. They aren't like Spanish Oaks or Antelope Valley or River Reaches: expensive places that had rotten water rights and turned to dust, money or no, when Vegas and L.A. put in their calls. And they didn't have to bail out of Phoenix Metro when the Central Arizona Project got turned off and then had its aqueducts blown to smithereens when Arizona wouldn't stop pumping out of Lake Mead.

Pouring water into Maggie's water trough, and looking around at his dusty patch with Annie out in the fields, Lolo reminds himself how lucky he is. He hasn't blown away. He and Annie are dug in. Calies may call them water ticks, but fuck them. If it weren't for people like him and Annie, they'd dry up and blow away the same as everyone else. And if Lolo moves a little bit of tamarisk around, well, the Calies deserve it, considering what they've done to everyone else.

Finished with Maggie, Lolo goes into the house and gets a drink of his own out of the filter urn. The water is cool in the shadows of the adobe house. Juniper beams hang low overhead. He sits down and connects his BuRec camera to the solar panel they've got scabbed onto the roof. Its charge light blinks amber. Lolo goes and gets some more water. He's used to being thirsty, but for some reason he can't get enough today. Big Daddy Drought's got his hands around Lolo's neck today.

Annie comes in, wiping her forehead with a tanned arm. "Don't drink too much water," she says. "I haven't been able to pump. Bunch of guardies around."

"What the hell are they doing around? We haven't even opened our headgates yet."

"They said they were looking for you."

Lolo almost drops his cup.

They know.

They know about his tamarisk reseeding. They know he's been splitting and planting root-clusters. That he's been dragging big healthy chunks of tamarisk up and down the river. A week ago he uploaded his claim on the canyon tamarisk—his biggest stand yet—almost worth an acre-foot in itself in water bounty. And now the guardies are knocking on his door.

Lolo forces his hand not to shake as he puts his cup down. "They say what they want?" He's surprised his voice doesn't crack.

"Just that they wanted to talk to you." She pauses. "They had one of those Humvees. With the guns."

Lolo closes his eyes. Forces himself to take a deep breath. "They've always got guns. It's probably nothing."

"It reminded me of Lake Havasu. When they cleared us out. When they shut down the water treatment plant and everyone tried to burn down the BLM office."

"It's probably nothing." Suddenly he's glad he never told her about his tamarisk hijinks. They can't punish her the same. How many acre-feet is he liable for? It must be hundreds. They'll want him, all right. Put him on a Straw work crew and make him work for life, repay his water debt forever. He's replanted hundreds, maybe thousands of tamarisk, shuffling them around like a cardsharp on a poker table, moving them from one bank to another, killing them again and again and again, and always happily sending in his "evidence."

"It's probably nothing," he says again.

"That's what people said in Havasu."

Lolo waves out at their newly tilled patch. The sun shines down hot and hard on the small plot. "We're not worth that kind of effort." He forces a grin. "It probably has to do with those enviro crazies who tried to blow up the Straw. Some of them supposedly ran this way. It's probably that."

Annie shakes her head, unconvinced. "I don't know. They could have asked me the same as you."

"Yeah, but I cover a lot of ground. See a lot of things. I'll bet that's why they want to talk to me. They're just looking for eco-freaks."

"Yeah, maybe you're right. It's probably that." She nods slowly, trying to make herself believe. "Those enviros, they don't make any sense at all. Not enough water for people, and they want to give the river to a bunch of fish and birds."

Lolo nods emphatically and grins wider. "Yeah. Stupid." But suddenly he views the eco-crazies with something approaching brotherly affection. The Californians are after him, too.

Lolo doesn't sleep all night. His instincts tell him to run, but he doesn't have the heart to tell Annie, or to leave her. He goes out in the morning hunting tamarisk and fails at that as well. He doesn't cut a single stand all day. He considers shooting himself with his shotgun, but chickens out when he gets the barrels in his mouth. Better alive and on the run than dead. Finally, as he stares into the twin barrels, he knows that he has to tell Annie, tell her he's been a water thief for years and that he's got to run north. Maybe she'll come with him. Maybe she'll see reason. They'll run together. At least they have that. For sure, he's not going to let those bastards take him off to a labor camp for the rest of his life.

But the guardies are already waiting when Lolo gets back. They're squatting in the shade of their Humvee, talking. When Lolo comes over the crest of the hill, one of them taps the other and points. They both stand. Annie is out in the field again, turning over dirt, unaware of what's about to happen. Lolo reins in and studies the guardies. They lean against their Humvee and watch him back.

Suddenly Lolo sees his future. It plays out in his mind the way it does in a movie, as clear as the blue sky above. He puts his hand on his shotgun. Where it sits on Maggie's far side, the guardies can't see it. He keeps Maggie angled away from them and lets the camel start down the hill.

The guardies saunter toward him. They've got their Humvee with a .50 caliber on the back and they've both got M-16s slung over their shoulders. They're in full bulletproof gear and they look flushed and hot. Lolo rides down slowly. He'll have to hit them both in the face. Sweat trickles between his shoulder blades. His hand is slick on the shotgun's stock.

The guardies are playing it cool. They've still got their rifles slung, and they let Lolo keep approaching. One of them has a wide smile. He's maybe 40 years old, and tanned. He's been out for a while, picking up a tan like that. The other raises a hand and says, "Hey there, Lolo."

Lolo's so surprised he takes his hand off his shotgun. "Hale?" He recognizes the guardie. He grew up with him. They played football together a million years ago, when football fields still had green grass and sprinklers sprayed their water straight into the air. Hale. Hale Perkins. Lolo scowls. He can't shoot Hale.

Hale says. "You're still out here, huh?"

"What the hell are you doing in that uniform? You with the Calies now?"

Hale grimaces and points to his uniform patches: Utah National Guard.

Lolo scowls. Utah National Guard. Colorado National Guard. Arizona National Guard. They're all the same. There's hardly a single member of the "National Guard" that isn't an out-of-state mercenary. Most of the local guardies quit a long time ago, sick to death of goose-stepping family and friends off their properties and sick to death of trading potshots with people who just wanted to stay in their homes. So even if there's still a Colorado National Guard, or an Arizona or a Utah, inside those uniforms with all their expensive nightsight gear and their brand-new choppers flying the river bends, it's pure California.

And then there are a few like Hale.

Lolo remembers Hale as being an OK guy. Remembers stealing a keg of beer from behind the Elks Club one night with him. Lolo eyes him. "How you liking that Supplementary Assistance Program?" He glances at the other guardie. "That working real well for you? The Calies a big help?"

Hale's eyes plead for understanding. "Come on, Lolo. I'm not like you. I got a family to look after. If I do another year of duty, they let Shannon and the kids base out of California."

"They give you a swimming pool in your backyard, too?"

"You know it's not like that. Water's scarce there, too."

Lolo wants to taunt him, but his heart isn't in it. A part of him wonders if Hale is just smart. At first, when California started winning its water lawsuits and shutting off cities, the displaced people just followed the water—right to California. It took a little while before the bureaucrats realized what was going on, but finally someone with a sharp pencil did the math and realized that taking in people along with their water didn't solve a water shortage. So the immigration fences went up.

But people like Hale can still get in.

"So what do you two want?" Inside, Lolo's wondering why

they haven't already pulled him off Maggie and hauled him away, but he's willing to play this out.

The other guardie grins. "Maybe we're just out here seeing how the water ticks live."

Lolo eyes him. This one, he could shoot. He lets his hand fall to his shotgun again. "BuRec sets my headgate. No reason for you to be out here."

The Calie says, "There were some marks on it. Big ones."

Lolo smiles tightly. He knows which marks the Calie is talking about. He made them with five different wrenches when he tried to dismember the entire headgate apparatus in a fit of obsession. Finally he gave up trying to open the bolts and just beat on the thing, banging the steel of the gate, smashing at it, while on the other side he had plants withering. After that, he gave up and just carried buckets of water to his plants and left it at that. But the dents and nicks are still there, reminding him of a period of madness. "It still works, don't it?"

Hale holds up a hand to his partner, quieting him. "Yeah, it still works. That's not why we're here."

"So what do you two want? You didn't drive all the way out here with your machine gun just to talk about dents in my headgate."

Hale sighs, put-upon, trying to be reasonable. "You mind getting down off that damn camel so we can talk?"

Lolo studies the two guardies, figuring his chances on the ground. "Shit." He spits. "Yeah, OK. You got me." He urges Maggie to kneel and climbs off her hump. "Annie didn't know anything about this. Don't get her involved. It was all me."

Hale's brow wrinkles, puzzled. "What are you talking about?"

"You're not arresting me?"

The Calie with Hale laughs. "Why? Cause you take a couple buckets of water from the river? Cause you probably got an illegal cistern around here somewhere?" He laughs again. "You ticks are all the same. You think we don't know about all that crap?"

Hale scowls at the Calie, then turns back to Lolo. "No, we're not here to arrest you. You know about the Straw?"

"Yeah." Lolo says it slowly, but inside, he's grinning. A great weight is suddenly off him. They don't know. They don't know shit. It was a good plan when he started it, and it's a good plan still. Lolo schools his face to keep the glee off, and tries to listen to what Hale's saying, but he can't, he's jumping up and down and gibbering like a monkey. They don't know—

"Wait." Lolo holds up his hand. "What did you just say?"

Hale repeats himself. "California's ending the water bounty. They've got enough Straw sections built up now that they don't need the program. They've got half the river enclosed. They got an agreement from the Department of Interior to focus their budget on seep and evaporation control. That's where all the big benefits are. They're shutting down the water bounty payout program." He pauses. "I'm sorry, Lolo."

Lolo frowns. "But a tamarisk is still a tamarisk. Why should one of those damn plants get the water? If I knock out a tamarisk, even if Cali doesn't want the water, I could still take it. Lots of people could use the water."

Hale looks pityingly at Lolo. "We don't make the regulations, we just enforce them. I'm supposed to tell you that your headgate won't get opened next year. If you keep hunting tamarisk, it won't do any good." He looks around the patch, then shrugs. "Anyway, in another couple years they were going to pipe this whole stretch. There won't be any tamarisk at all after that."

"What am I supposed to do, then?"

"California and BuRec is offering early buyout money." Hale pulls a booklet out of his bulletproof vest and flips it open. "Sort of to soften the blow." The pages of the booklet flap in the hot breeze. Hale pins the pages with a thumb and pulls a pen out of another vest pocket. He marks something on the booklet, then tears off a perforated check. "It's not a bad deal."

Lolo takes the check. Stares at it. "Five hundred dollars?"

Hale shrugs sadly. "It's what they're offering. That's just the paper codes. You confirm it online. Use your BuRec camera phone, and they'll deposit it in whatever bank you want. Or they can hold it in trust until you get into a town and want to withdraw it. Any place with a BLM office, you can do that. But you need to confirm before April 15. Then BuRec'll send out a guy to shut down your headgate before this season gets going."

"Five hundred dollars?"

"It's enough to get you north. That's more than they're offering next year."

"But this is my patch."

"Not as long as we've got Big Daddy Drought. I'm sorry, Lolo."

"The drought could break any time. Why can't they give us

a couple more years? It could break any time." But even as he says it, Lolo doesn't believe. Ten years ago, he might have. But not now. Big Daddy Drought's here to stay. He clutches the check and its keycodes to his chest.

A hundred yards away, the river flows on to California.

TIME CAPSULE FOUND ON THE DEAD PLANET

by Margaret Atwood

1.

In the first age, we created gods. We carved them out of wood; there was still such a thing as wood, then. We forged them from shining metals and painted them on temple walls. They were gods of many kinds, and goddesses as well. Sometimes they were cruel and drank our blood, but also they gave us rain and sunshine, favorable winds, good harvests, fertile animals, many children. A million birds flew over us then, a million fish swam in our seas.

Our gods had horns on their heads, or moons, or sealey fins, or the beaks of eagles. We called them All-Knowing, we called them Shining One. We knew we were not orphans. We smelled the earth and rolled in it; its juices ran down our chins.

2.

In the second age we created money. This money was also made of shining metals. It had two faces: on one side was a severed head, that of a king or some other noteworthy person, on the other face was something else, something that would give us comfort: a bird, a fish, a fur-bearing animal. This was all that remained of our former gods. The money was small in size, and each of us would carry some of it with him every day, as close to the skin as possible. We could not eat this money, wear it or burn it for warmth; but as if by magic it could be changed into such things. The money was mysterious, and we were in awe of it. If you had enough of it, it was said, you would be able to fly.

3.

In the third age, money became a god. It was all-powerful, and out of control. It began to talk. It began to create on its own. It created feasts and famines, songs of joy, lamentations. It created greed and hunger, which were its two faces. Towers of glass rose at its name, were destroyed and rose again. It began to eat things. It ate whole forests, croplands, and the lives of children. It ate armies, ships and cities. No one could stop it. To have it was a sign of grace.

4.

In the fourth age we created deserts. Our deserts were of several kinds, but they had one thing in common: nothing grew there. Some were made of cement, some were made of various poisons, some of baked earth. We made these deserts from the desire for more money and from despair at the lack of it. Wars, plagues and famines visited us, but we did not stop in our industrious creation of deserts. At last all wells were poisoned, all rivers ran with filth, all seas were dead; there was no land left to grow food.

Some of our wise men turned to the contemplation of deserts. A stone in the sand in the setting sun could be very beautiful, they said. Deserts were tidy, because there were no weeds in them, nothing that crawled. Stay in the desert long enough, and you could apprehend the absolute. The number zero was holy.

5.

You who have come here from some distant world, to this dry lakeshore and this cairn, and to this cylinder of brass, in which on the last day of all our recorded days I place our final words:

Pray for us, who once, too, thought we could fly.

CONTRIBUTORS

MARGARET ATWOOD is a Booker Prize–winning poet and author of many acclaimed novels, including *The Blind Assassin* and *The Handmaid's Tale*.

PAOLO BACIGALUPI is the author of the sci-fi novel *The Wind-Up Girl*, which won the Hugo and Nebula awards. "The Tamarisk Hunter" was published in his 2010 collection *Pump Six and Other Stories* (Night Shade Books).

T. C. BOYLE has a long list of books to his credit, including the PEN/Faulkner Award–winning novel *World's End* and *The Road to Wellville*. His latest novel is *When the Killing's Done* (Viking Adult).

TOBY LITT has written nine novels and two short story collections; in 2003 he was chosen as one of *Granta's* twenty Best British Novelists Under Forty.

LYDIA MILLET won the 2003 PEN-USA Award for her third novel, *My Happy Life*, and her short story collection *Love in*

Infant Monkeys was one of three finalists for the 2010 Pulitzer Prize. Her latest novel, *Ghost Lights*, is due November 2011 from W. W. Norton.

DAVID MITCHELL has been twice shortlisted for the Booker Prize; his novels include *Cloud Atlas* and most recently *The Thousand Autumns of Jacob de Zoet* (Random House). "The Siphoners" has not previously been published.

NATHANIEL RICH is the author of *The Mayor's Tongue*; his second novel, *Odds Against Tomorrow*, is forthcoming from Farrar, Straus and Giroux. "Hermie" was published by *Night & Day* in 2011.

HELEN SIMPSON is a prize-winning short story writer and novelist; in 1993, she was selected as one of *Granta*'s twenty Best British Novelists Under Forty.

KIM STANLEY ROBINSON is the Hugo and Nebula prize–winning author of the Mars Trilogy and a trilogy of novels about climate change that go under the title Science in the Capital. The story here is adapted from the third novel in the latter trilogy, *Sixty Days and Counting*.

WU MING 1 is one fourth of the Italian writers' collective Wu Ming, authors of *Q* and *Manituana* (Verso). "Arzèstul" has not previously been published in English, but appears in the short-story collections *Anteprima nazionale. Nove visioni del nostro futuro invisibile* (Minimum Fax 2009) and *Anatra all'arancia meccanica* (Clockwork Duck à l'Orange 2011). The story is dedicated to Graziano Manzoni.

350.org is building a global grassroots movement to solve the climate crisis. Our online campaigns, grassroots organizing, and mass public actions are led from the bottom up by thousands of volunteer organizers in over 188 countries.

350 means climate safety. To preserve our planet, scientists tell us we must reduce the amount of CO_2 in the atmosphere from its current level of 392 parts per million to below 350 ppm. But 350 is more than a number—it's a symbol of where we need to head as a planet.

350.org works hard to organize in a new way—everywhere at once, using online tools to facilitate strategic offline action. We want to be a laboratory for the best ways to strengthen the climate movement and catalyze transformation around the world.

We think we can turn the tide on the climate crisis—but only if we work together. If an international grassroots movement holds our leaders accountable to realities of science and principles of justice, we can realize the solutions that will ensure a better future for all.

350.org

organizers@350.org

www.350.org